We are never alone.

8ᵗʰ December 1980

John Lennon Dies, So Do I

The day I died was the exact same day John Lennon was shot by some crazy fan outside the Dakota building, across from Central Park. This psycho loved the ex-Beatle so much he decided to show him, not with the normal round of applause you may expect, but a round of bullets straight into his chest.

But unlike John's death mine was your standard run of the mill, number one killing degenerative disease in America—a heart attack, that went pretty much unnoticed.

So there I was at home on the driveway washing the car thinking about how life had been quite good to me, apart from a few near escapes in the fire department, feeling pretty pleased about what I had achieved. My ladder company had saved quite a few lives, my family was doing well and we all lived in a nice house in Queens. Nothing fancy but nice.

Then suddenly I felt this sharp pain in my chest. I bent over as a natural response to stop it happening and the next thing I know I'm hovering over my body that has fallen to the floor. No pain anymore. Just confusion. Was I dying? At fifty-two, I hoped not. Matt and Luke my two sons came out to help me. They must have been watching. Then a seductive, blinding light came down behind me beckoning me to go to it. The pull of its energy was so strong but I couldn't go. Not yet. Not until I knew there was no way of getting back into my body and back to my family.

We've all been there. Every one of us up here has been through it and every one of you down there will have to go through it too. The King, Miss Monroe, Gandhi, JFK, you name it, everyone.

Death comes to us all eventually but it's just an illusion. It's all an illusion. It's not that bad honestly. In fact it can be kinda liberating in many ways. Once the cloak of life, which is the body, has fallen, we no longer need to feed it, clothe it, house it and keep it healthy. Basic survival takes up so much of our Earthly energy. Once this has gone an enormous amount of spiritual energy is freed up. Ultimately death is spiritual freedom.

Matt screamed for his mom, my wife Win, who came running hysterically.

"Dial 911," she cried.

Luke took one look, then did the older brother bit, and took charge. Matt, at only eleven years old, was in total shock and didn't know what to do.

In the ambulance I was still there, aware of everything, following my body as it was carted off to emergency. A couple of guys bent over me and looked like they were trying to get my heart going again first with their hands, then with machines. I couldn't feel anything because I wasn't in it anymore. Quite where I was I wasn't sure. Out of the window I could see Win, Luke and Matt following us.

It's such a shock to find yourself in this position in the back of an ambulance just watching and hoping they will revive you, even though you feel totally alive. I felt anxious but calm and light too. Very strange.

There was a long whistling noise.

"He's gone," one of the guys said and sat back down.

"Don't worry it must have been his time," the other one said.

"If you're still hanging around trying to get back into your body man

6

then I'm afraid it's game over. Your body don't want you no more. You have to cross over. Just go towards the light and you'll be taken care of," he said looking into space.

"Are you talking to me?" I said.

"Yeah, I'm talking to you," he replied.

"You're lucky, buddy, you've got a psychic paramedic. A lot of the others just don't have a clue, according to my partner here," said his colleague, sounding like a non-believer. "But we don't tell anyone, do we Dean?"

"No, the world's not ready for this quite yet," Dean said.

I followed my body up to a point then decided I'd better find my family. In the corridor of the hospital, I could see all sorts of crazy things that I won't even go into now, but I could also see my son Matt coming out of the relatives only room with tears in his eyes. He ran down the corridor so I ran after him.

Outside the hospital, he lifted his arms up towards the sky and shouted "Nooooooooooooo!"

I was right beside him. If only he had known at that time that I wasn't really dead. How different his life would have been if he knew that death is not really the end, it's just the beginning, of an amazing adventure.

September 11th 2001

2:45AM

"Don't let them see us," whispered Delilah, my new companion who had just completed training in the spirit world to become a guide.

Delilah is a large African lady, splashed in color and jewellery from head to toe, aged about forty-five and is the most vibrant spirit woman I have ever seen, with the personality to match.

"They can't see us, we're dead," I replied looking across Matt and Rowena's bedroom in their trendy Greenwich Village home on lower Manhattan's west side.

Rowena is beautiful in many ways with long, black curly hair cascading down her back. She puts Matt's once muscular physique to shame with her several years younger, yoga toned body. While he is sitting up bare chested, leaning up against the headboard of their antique, hand-carved bed, he reveals nothing but a hairy chest and a birthmark, shaped like a bullet wound. Rowena is sleeping in one of his old shirts with her back turned to him and my son, who has inherited my Italian olive skin and dark wavy hair, is glancing over charts and graphs. September 11th is an important deadline for him.

"My Rowena is very perceptive. She sees things you know," Delilah said taking ownership of Rowena, as she was once related to her way back in the family tree.

"No she doesn't," I replied knowing that it was more wishful thinking on Delilah's part. Rowena wanted to see things but she didn't actually see anything. She thought being psychic might help in her work as a homeopath. And for those of you who don't know what a homeopath is, as I didn't, it's alternative medicine involving white pills and different vibrations. Let's just leave it at that.

Unbeknown to Matt and Rowena, myself and Delilah spend a lot of time in their bedroom while they are asleep and we had just zipped through the open window and started to materialise ourselves into more solid shapes. First the wiggly lines come, then, like in the beam me up Scotty scenes in *Star Trek*, we become more solid. I always project my astral image at a much younger, fitter age than the day I died.

"She's not going to see anything when she's asleep," I said.

"Have you forgotten the inbetweeny state?" Delilah replied. She was referring to the state in between asleep and awake where you fall off walls and wake up with a jolt. It is in this state that a person's psychic perception is heightened and a lot of guides use it to get messages across through dreams.

The clock on the bedside table said 2:45am.

"How do you turn these damn alarm clocks off?" Delilah quizzed. "In my time on Earth we just used to get up at sunrise," she said thinking back to her last life as a slave.

"Why do you wanna do that?" I asked her.

"I was at the meeting. I was trying to get your attention honey but, no, head well and truly in the clouds. Rowena might be in danger. She can't go near the World Trade Center tomorrow. She has to stay home," she explained.

"What you talking about? The meeting isn't until 3:00am Earth time," I corrected.

"I went early."

"But you're not supposed to do that on the Earth plane!"

"No-one told *me*." Delilah sounded defensive.

"It's in **The Earth Guide Book**."

Delilah took her guide book out of her pocket and started flicking frantically through the pages until it landed on the chapter that said "Rules for Guides". Delilah read out loud:

"It is requested that unless an absolute cosmic emergency occurs all guides must refrain from projecting themselves into the future on the Earth plane for their own gain." Delilah looked embarrassed.

"I told you," I said trying not to feel smug.

"Oh well, I've done it now but I won't tell you what happened. Just tell me how to switch this alarm clock off...oh I got it partner." Delilah closed the book on the section that told her how to move physical matter. "Cover me, I'm going down."

I rolled my eyes as she pretended to be a TV cop—something I'd noticed she liked doing often. Delilah started to become even more solid because in order to move physical objects spirits have to lower their vibration to gain entry into the physical world. Depending on the amount of experience a spirit has determines how much they can influence matter.

As she lowered her vibration and reached across to the clock she knocked a large pile of books which slowly wobbled, like a tower undecided as to which way to fall. I quickly zoomed in lowering my vibration fast to try and help but it was too late and they crashed to the floor.

"Oh sugar!" Delilah half shouted, half whispered.

Strewn across the floor were all Rowena's books with titles like "*Love, Sex and Intimacy*", "*A Guide to Homeopathy*" and "*Men are from Mars, Women are from Venus*".

Delilah also dropped her copy of **The Earth Guide Book** and as it landed on the Earth plane it too became a solid physical object and its pages flipped open revealing the words:

**"When it feels like your world is falling apart
this is a time of great spiritual growth."**

Rowena didn't stir but Matt looked up from his papers, over his half-moon glasses which made him look much older than the thirty-two years he was. Reluctantly he got out of bed revealing a beer belly that used to be a six pack he was proud of. One too many visits to *Starbucks* and an expired gym membership hadn't done him any favours.

"What's this nonsense?" he muttered to himself as he looked at the cover of one of the books, totally unaware of what Rowena was reading. As he finished putting them all back on the side table I put the thought in his head to take one with him. He did. It was the guide book.

"Oh no, he's taken my guide book," Delilah shrieked.

"You'd have a job getting that back anyway. Once it becomes solid it's normally lost to the Earth plane forever," I replied.

Matt headed down the dark corridor. He knew to head towards the light at the end which was a journey to the bathroom he'd done a million times before. In the background the night buzz of the city could be heard with the occasional police siren whirring, dogs barking, the odd truck going passed but on the whole it was pretty damn quiet for New York.

The alarm clock switch glided to the off position as Delilah took the opportunity to use all her mental and spiritual capabilities to move it. She looked pleased with herself when it was done.

"If you wanna good job doing then ask a woman," she said. "Isn't that right Rowena?" Rowena was dead to the world.

I found Matt sitting on the toilet with the book already tossed on the floor. "You should read that son it might help you," I projected. These thoughts flashed across his mind and he picked the book back up. He read the cover which said **The Earth Guide Book—think of the problem, open the book and there will be your answer.**

"Yeah right," he said and threw it back down.

It fell open to the words:

"Dying is one of the most amazing spiritual experiences you will ever have. Enjoy it if you can."

Matt raised his eyebrows and shook his head in disagreement before heading back to bed.

3:00AM

The New York City skyline silhouettes and shapes itself like a picture postcard. Street lights, car headlights, shops, restaurants, apartments all twinkle their life into the darkness. But as I make the familiar flight across the sky there is an additional light hovering brightly over lower Manhattan. Electrical sparks of multicolored energy, some red, some blue, some purple, some white, some pink are all making their way towards this beacon, myself included.

A meeting had been summoned for all the spirit guides serving the people in the city of New York.

The meeting was scheduled for 3:00am, Earth time, in the middle elevator lobby of the north tower of the World Trade Center. Rumours were flying around that tomorrow the city was going to be hit by one of the most terrifying experiences America had ever known.

The twin towers stood majestically above the city like infinitely long legs of some concrete giant. I had been there thousands of times with Matt, accompanying him to work. And now on this mild September night flying felt fantastic. A real sense of freedom. I couldn't ever imagine having a body again or even wanting one as I zipped over The Port Authority Buildings, The Woolworth Building and The Millennium Hilton towards the meeting.

As I approached the window of the north tower, lit by security lights, I suddenly had a strange flash in my third eye which was accompanied by a sinking feeling in my energy field. I saw for a very minute instant the window, that I was about to pass through, shattering into thousands of tiny pieces. This would be by the force of a Boeing 737 later that morning, but I didn't know it yet. All I knew was something sinister was around the corner.

I landed in the large elevator lobby that housed many of the super fast, almost turbocharged lifts which fed the workers into the tower each day. A silent energy hummed all around as thousands of guides stood, waiting expectantly. This was an unusual sight to see so many guides in one place. They all had their special qualities and gifts they had chosen to give back to the Earth plane, where they mostly acquired them from in the first place.

I landed and formed myself into my own Earthly identity—Jonathan Moretti, aged 52—as I was on the Earth plane the day I died. Slowly I materialised into shape for the second time this evening.

One of the smaller guides, with angelic looking features, was hanging half in, half out of the closed window, like he was doing a magic show, on the lookout for one of the greatest beings in existence in the entire cosmos.

"She's coming," he shouted fluttering his tiny wings to move himself back in through the window.

The vibe in the room lifted as spirits started to feel excited about being in her presence, as she was showered in heavenly golden light, and all of us would be bathed in it very soon. I had only met her once and that was beyond words. Her vibration was so high, pure love.

All heads turned to see a very bright, search beam type light making its way across the sky, from the Statue of Liberty, in the distance. Calmly, intently and with real purpose. She was indeed on her way.

Nobody knew what to call her as she had no name and was really neither male nor female. Once you progress through the spiritual world gender becomes less and less important. For the sake of identity she had been nicknamed "Doris".

All those gathered in the lobby just watched as she approached the building. A hue of golden purple light became clearer as it neared the tower. Doris started to morph into the shape of an angel. Large wings spread long and wide across her back she flapped in greeting to the two watchers hanging through the window. She was accompanied by two smaller angelic presences. All three, Doris first, glided into the north tower landing graciously in front of her captive audience. She looked around the room, up and down at the ceiling and floor, across from side to side at the walls which were temporarily bricking them in, sensing where she was and how it would be later that morning. Once ready she turned to her mesmerised audience and said,

"Spirit friends thank you for being here."

The energy of love filled the room. She was just as amazing as I remembered her. Everyone was silent.

"It is no coincidence that you have been called here and it is no coincidence that some of your Earth friends will be leaving their bodies very soon."

A few spirits mumbled some things energetically to each other.

"Tomorrow morning an attack, which will be deemed by the world to be of a terrorist origin, will take place here, on this building. At precisely 8:46am Earth time a hijacked plane will crash into this very building between the 94th and 98th floors. The space you are occupying now will become a tomb for hundreds of people. These people need you."

A spirit guide indicated through his aura that he wanted to ask a question but Doris sent out a vibration which told him to wait a moment.

"Almost twenty minutes later a second plane will hit the south tower at 9:03am between the 78th and 84th floors. The people in this tower and the people of New York will be gripped with fear."

"Remember everyone on this planet, including those involved in the disaster are here because they chose to be and although they do not always remember it they are spiritual beings having a human experience.

Not the other way round. And their higher selves will know where they are headed whether that means death of the physical body or continuing on this Earth plane."

Everyone was listening intently.

"All of you have an Earthly friend or relative that is either in danger or who will be coming home tomorrow. You need to know what their higher selves have chosen so you can guide them appropriately."

Just for the record the higher self is the part of the individual that knows everything and is in tune with its own spiritual growth and development.

I felt a mixture of fear and excitement when I heard this news. Fear for the morning's terrible events and the suffering that would have to be endured by thousands of innocent people, my son included, but part excitement that Matt might be coming home and that we would see each other again. It had been a long time.

Doris put her wings up high into the lobby area and said,

"Please form two groups. Group one over here,"—she pointed with her wing—"and group two over there."

I was strongly drawn to group one and hovered over to the area pointed out by Doris. It took a matter of seconds for the 3000 or so spirit guides to move into place. I noticed Delilah in group two.

As everyone settled down and the energy in the room silenced again Doris announced,

"Group One, your Earth friends will be passing over tomorrow and you must guide them safely back home. Group Two, your friends will be in danger and you must guide them away from New York's financial district."

Oh my goodness! I remembered how hard it was for my children, especially Matt, when I left the Earth plane. Tomorrow would be a strange repeat of history. Like going back in time somehow. I knew it was my job to make it better for Matt and his family, but at this point I wished I hadn't volunteered to be his guide. I wasn't sure if I could do it. Couldn't I save him?

"There is no point trying to keep your loved ones here because it has already been decided what will be. You cannot change it now. It is too late for that. Your job is to make it better in whatever way possible," Doris said as though reading my mind. "Remember it is the higher self of every human being that is the guiding force through life. They know where they are heading."

Doris left a warm glow of love and support in the room as she exited back through the window across the West Side highway, Battery Park and the Hudson River back towards the great lady of liberty standing guard over New York.

3:10AM

Rowena is in the Trade Center. She looks down at her hands. They are covered in blood. She presses the 'going up' button for the elevator and smears blood all over the wall. Her feet are also bleeding. She is inside the elevator squashed tight. She looks around at the people beside her and their faces turn into faces of zombies. "Aaaaaaaaaaaaah!" she screams.

Delilah was above Rowena's third eye sending her these images and whilst she was busy doing that I decided it would be a good idea for Matt, who was now asleep, to have **The Earth Guide Book** with him tomorrow. So I was using all my psychic power to move the book from the side of his bed, across the room, to the deep folds of his suit pocket, which was hanging neatly on the back of the wardrobe door.

The book juddered, like an old car engine getting going, as it lifted off the table, then like a humming bird, it glided across the room. The amount of mental focus I needed to move just one fairly light object was enormous.

As the book was in mid-flight Rowena suddenly woke up with a start. "Don't take the elevator," Delilah said firmly. The words "don't take the elevator" came into Rowena's mind.

I looked across anxiously wondering whether or not she would notice the now very physical **Earth Guide Book** which was hanging in mid-air. But fortunately she didn't. Instead she turned and cuddled Matt's safe body for a few moments before she became more interested in the clock which said 3:10am.

"That can't be right," she thought. She felt like she'd only been asleep for a minute. On examining the clock Rowena noticed the alarm had been switched off, much to Delilah's frustration she turned it back on.

7:35AM

September 11th, a beautiful sunny morning with not a cloud in the sky. *The New York Times* weather section predicted the temperatures to land somewhere between 66°F and 79°F. Already the city was crawling with workers preparing for a day, that unbeknown to them, would go down in history as one of the worst days in America.

"Jakey get up sweetheart, we're late," Rowena shouted into his room as she buttoned up her blouse.

Jake, their youngest, at only ten, was already lying awake and in his cool, automobile-shaped bed. Tears rolled down his face.

"Get up Jakey we're...hey, what's the matter?" she asked as she popped her head round the door and noticed his upset.

"I just had a dream about dad. I dreamt that he died from smoke," he stuttered quite shaken. It had obviously disturbed him. I nodded at Jake's guide Tonto, a Native American sitting in the corner. Jake had tapped into the future through his dreams. He often had prophetic dreams without realising it.

"Oh baby. Daddy is okay. He's in his office," she said trying to reassure him, squeezing him tight, with the type of comforting squeeze, that only his mom could give him.

"Why we late anyway?" he said.

"Faulty alarm clock," she replied. Delilah couldn't help but grin.

Rowena was a great mother and wife, Matt had done well for himself. She was very committed to her family, with great family values that she'd tried to instil into her two beautiful children from a very early age. She wanted them to be happy and when this goal was achieved it meant she could be happy too. Her therapist friend Cathy, however, thought this was not a good idea as allowing yourself to be happy only when others are happy was surely a ticket to certain misery. So Rowena was working on this.

"I don't wanna go to school today mom. I don't feel well," Jake groaned.

"You'll be just fine once you get going baby. It's important to go to school. You've got exams soon and you don't wanna miss anything."

The next stop was Tom's room. A typical fifteen-year-old's pad that smelled like he'd been hanging out of the window smoking half the night. Pictures of big-breasted blonde beauties, from cheer leaders to pop stars, were all over his walls. She hoped these women were as appalled as she was at the absolute dump he called his room.

Rowena made her way across the obstacle course to the window and opened the curtains kinda roughly. "Wake up Tom. You got half an hour," she shouted.

"What?" he cried leaping out of bed. "I haven't done my hair." It took Tom the longest time to get ready because of his vanity and spiky hair-do that he meticulously groomed for hours in the morning. Today it was even more necessary as he planned to ask out Laura, the girl he'd been in love with for months.

"You're not going out this weekend mister if you don't tidy this room up by then," she said hoping the threat might motivate him to clean it. But he knew she wouldn't follow through and her comments just washed over him as he headed for the shower.

Finally she went into the office where Matt was sitting at a computer poring over his assessments smoking a cigarette. He'd been there since six.

"Didn't you think to wake us up?" she said angrily. As far as Rowena was concerned this was almost the final nail in the coffin of a very bad month of Matt's "couldn't care less" behaviour.

"I didn't know you were late!"

"Why does that not surprise me?"

"Don't blame me! You got an alarm clock!"

"Yes but it didn't go off and now I'm running half an hour late and I've gotta get the boys to school on time."

My son didn't look up from his computer screen which annoyed her even more.

"Men are from Mars. You're from a different solar system all together. Matt I'm talking to you," she shouted.

He was forced to look up but wasn't impressed.

"You know I've got my yearly assessment this morning," he said firmly, reaching for another cigarette, the third one of the morning.

"Smoking isn't gonna help," she continued.

"It does!"

"Do you know what you're doing to your kids?"

"What you talking about? I never smoke near them."

"Jake was in tears this morning. He dreamt you smoked yourself to death. Even the kids are worried about you!"

"I'm fine. I'm happy smoking," he lied. He hated smoking and I knew he hated himself for not being able to give up.

"You can't ignore the warnings on TV. You'll end up with cancer. Then where will we be?"

"Is that supposed to make me feel better?" he said starting to get irritated. This was his biggest fear.

"I'm just worried about you honey," her voice softened because she didn't want to push him too far as she knew the consequences.

23

"Look, don't start. Not today. It's a big day. I'll give up when the time's right," he said sitting on his anger.

Downstairs, in their blue and pink kitchen which had photographic stills of different areas of New York on one wall and nutritional charts on the other, Jake was waiting at the breakfast table. Rowena always insisted that everyone eat together at meal times to keep the family bonded and safe. She'd read it in one of her self-help books and it did work. It was Matt she had the most trouble with.

Jake was playing with a model airplane he'd made and was flying it around the table like a fighter plane bombing the marmalade, the jam, the milk, the toast and the final target, the cornflakes.

"Eeeeeeeeeeeeeeeooooooooooooooooow crash," he sang as he nose-dived into the cornflake box sending them everywhere.

His dad walked in at just the wrong moment.

"Jake, for God's sake, what the hell do you think you're doing?" he shouted giving him a clip round the ear, an anger that was really meant for Rowena.

"Oooww," Jake screamed much louder than the clip warranted. He threw his airplane down on the floor with great force smashing its nose and breaking a wing then stormed off to his bedroom wailing. It was the shock and the force of his dad's voice that upset him more than anything.

There was nothing Tonto or I could do to stop the dynamics between them. We knew that this was not a good start to September 11th and there was not much time to rectify the situation, if any at all.

"Breakfast on the floor this morning then?" Tom said as he paraded into the kitchen like a dog back from the grooming parlour, leaving the TV blaring out Good Morning America in the living area.

"*You* can clear these up," Matt snapped stopping his task and pouring himself a cup of extra strong coffee.

"What? But dad I haven't even done anything. It's not *my* problem," Tom said in protest.

"Just do it Tom." Matt gave Tom a stern look.

As Tom started picking them up he muttered something under his breath, which was like a red rag to a bull to Matt. He hated it when his children rebelled, as I had done when he was a boy.

"What did you say?" he shouted.

"Chill man," Tom said. "What's your problem?"

"Right that's it. You're grounded this weekend," Matt fumed.

"But I've got a hot date," Tom said—optimistically because he hadn't actually asked her yet.

"Tough," his father replied.

"It's Laura Johnson. Her dad Brad Johnson works with you at the Trade Center, two floors down from heaven." Tom tried to appease him by using his dad's favourite phrase which described where he worked. He wasn't actually two floors down from the top but he was pretty high up on the 92nd floor of the south tower, only eighteen floors from the roof.

Rowena entered the room with Delilah following behind.

"What have you done to Jakey?" demanded Rowena, concerned about Matt's stressed out behaviour.

"It was a gentle tap that's all," he said in his defence. "I can't take any more of this. You're supposed to back me up."

Much to Tom's relief Matt stormed out of the kitchen without saying goodbye, leaving the extra briefcase with all his assessment papers in it by the table. Rowena followed him towards the front door.

"He loves you so much and he thinks you hate him," she said.

"I'll sort it out with him later. I've gotta get to work," he replied a little more calmly as he put his jacket on. "See you later."

"What time will you be home?"

"I dunno, depends how the day goes."

25

"I hope the assessment goes well." She tried ending on a positive note.

"Yeah thanks, I'll catch you later." Matt gave her a small mechanical peck on the cheek.

"You should give her a proper kiss and look her in the eyes because you might never see her again," I said projecting these thoughts into Matt's head. But as they flashed across his mind he dismissed them as rubbish, opened the door and left, embarking on his final journey to the Trade Center.

7:42 AM

As a spirit guide I am now able to transport my energies to any place, any time, in order to see what is happening elsewhere. This has taken much practice and is a damn sight easier without a body. Whilst still in a body, it is called psychic viewing and is very advanced for an Earth bound spirit.

I projected myself to Logan Airport, Boston, crossing the time and space barriers of the Earth plane.

"My son is picking me up. What about you?" An old woman made polite conversation to the lady next to her whilst waiting to go through the security scanner.

"Roy, my hubby will be there, I hope, if he remembers. He's getting forgetful," she replied as she stepped through. The buzzer went off.

"Damn that always happens to me."

A blue uniformed female, security officer approached with a hand held metal detector.

"It's my pacemaker, angel," she said pointing at her chest. The security woman placed the scanner over her heart and it made a sharp whistling noise.

"Okay you can go ma'am."

A sudden rush of calm ran through the building, which could only mean one thing—angels had just entered. From behind the crowds a light started emerging and before too long a picture formed of a white robed, golden glowing Doris, her wings expansive with a span of at least twenty feet.

Nobody without extrasensory perception would have noticed her as she walked, like a queen on her coronation day, through the crowds. Straight through the gateway of the x-ray machine and on into the waiting area, towards the passengers ready to board American Airlines flight 11 which was, unbeknown to them, about to take them to their final destination.

Doris was on another rescue mission and had been training and preparing her 70,000 strong spirit rescue team for years. Hovering slightly off the ground Doris looked over the shoulder of an airport attendant and compared their clipboard details to the one she had buried deep in her left wing.

"That's two pilots, seven flight attendants and I have only 56 passengers here, not 60. There will be a reason for that," she said to herself.

Another glamorous looking woman arrived. "We've had four cancellations this morning. They won't be making it. Their names are…"

Doris knew already that one got stuck on the subway, two overslept and one had been rushed to hospital with suspected appendicitis. She mentally praised the guides responsible for helping the passengers miss the plane.

"Okay all the right souls are here," she confirmed. "First team please take your positions amongst them."

As this was transmitted I saw a team of twenty white beings descend from out of nowhere just leaking through the ceiling of the airport. They dispersed themselves in and amongst the nervous passengers, cloaking them with loving protective energy to help soften the blow of what was about to happen.

7:43AM

The number one train downtown to Cortlandt Street, which dropped passengers virtually at the door of the Trade Center, via an underground concourse, was crawling with people.

Early morning rush hour was the part of Matt's day I looked forward to least. It's really hard work being a guide in the New York subway system, where vibrations are low and oppressive. This morning was no exception.

Most of the travellers were reading, either one of the free papers, that were shoved by the thousands into the fast paced city commuters' hands, or *The New York Times* or *Sun* or their own reading material such as documents, novels, magazines. In fact anything to avoid human contact.

Matt's work colleague Brad, a smartly dressed, blonde haired, chiselled faced guy with a clean white shirt and expensive green Macy's tie, was being uncomfortably pushed up against him. To hide his embarrassment he started making jokes.

"It feels so good to be so close to you again," he said quite loudly with a twinkling smile in his eyes making me laugh but not Matt.

Some of the passengers on the train looked round. There was a mixture of travellers, from the young black guy wearing baseball cap and hood up, to the suited financial district traders, to the long-skirted secretaries sporting sneakers and carrying their "proper shoes" in their day bags.

"Shut up Brad. I'm not in the mood for jokes today," he said with equal volume, feeling claustrophobic.

"Come on man lighten up. Life's too short to take it so seriously," Brad laughed.

I felt for Matt. He was even more anxious than usual about the day ahead. He was aware of his rising stress levels and wished he could be laid back and calm, like Brad, but on some level he also knew today was not just a big day in terms of work but a big day in terms of his entire existence. Subconsciously he knew something was going to happen.

As the train pulled out of Franklin Street station the passengers headed for darkness again, entering another very uninviting tunnel, which was just a tiny section of the sprawling New York subway that housed thousands of cables, wires, pipes and rats.

Matt spotted Tracey, a woman who works a few floors above him, and was glad of the crowds as he wanted to avoid any eye contact.

"Is that Tracey from 99?" Matt jumped.

"Yep, the eyes in the back of your head must be working well today," quipped Brad.

"Has she seen us?" Matt asked.

"Erm no. I don't think so," he replied.

Brad stood on his tiptoes to get a better look making himself look really conspicuous.

"Oh, erm, I think she has now," Brad kinda said apologetically.

"Good one Brad."

"Why what's up buddy?"

The lights flickered then went out for a few seconds sending the passengers into a brief but eerie silence, which was eventually relieved when they saw the brightness of the next station emerging at the other end.

"This is our stop," declared Matt and as the doors flew open they both rolled out with the crowd onto the platform that took them through the concourse to the World Trade Center.

"Quick Brad, keep up pace," Matt said. "I don't wanna talk to her."

"You got the hots for her or something?" Brad asked.

"No!" replied Matt.

"Don't you? I do. She's really hot."

"You're a married man." Matt sounded shocked.

"The eyes can look but the fingers don't touch." Brad was very loyal to his wife and family.

"Just don't look now okay? I'm stressed enough as it is."

"What is it with you man? Did you do her a bad deal?" Brad was curious.

"I'll tell you later." Matt quickened his stride to reach the entrance to the south tower.

"There were rumours flying around that some guy got her...you know," Brad gestured a balloon shape over his tummy sticking his pelvis out to avoid saying the word pregnant as though it was a dirty word or something, "...last Christmas and he had to face the wrath of her body-building boyfriend."

"Really," Matt said, pretending not to be interested.

As they entered World Trade Center 2 angels and spirit guides were everywhere, filling the building. But Matt and Brad had no idea. As far as they were concerned this was going to be just another normal day at work.

A young man in jeans raced towards us carrying what looked like the contents of his desk. He bumped into Matt causing **The Earth Guide Book** to drop out of his pocket.

"Hey watch it!...Patrick?" Matt recognised him. "What you doing? You leaving?"

"Oh err sorry Matt I didn't see you…err yes I'm afraid I got an e-mail from the big B last night telling me there wasn't a position for me anymore. My three month trial didn't work out I guess," he said.

"Oh I'm sorry. I always thought you were cruising along," encouraged Brad.

"Yeah me too but obviously not. I'm totally gutted man." Patrick struggled with his emotions.

"It's a bit short notice asking you to leave today," Matt commented.

"You'd have thought the bastard would have waited until after the assessments," Brad interjected.

"He said I could hang around another two paid weeks if I wanted but I'm outa here. I know when I'm not wanted. I'll see you around."

I looked at Patrick's guide, a young Chinese chap, who looked pleased with himself.

The Earth Guide Book was on the floor open to the words:

> **"When you're on Earth you just never know why things are happening. Even something that feels like the worst thing ever can turn out to be the best."**

"What's this buddy **The Earth Guide Book**?" Brad laughed as he picked it up.

"Where'd you find that?"

"You just dropped it."

"It'll be one of those stupid women's self-help, love yourself and the rest of the world type books Rowena's reading. How did that get there anyway? She must have sneaked it into my pocket hoping I'll read it, as if I haven't got enough to read," Matt said answering his own question.

It was a rewarding moment for me. All those years in sphere four of the spirit world learning to move physical objects had paid off.

Brad flicked through it and read,

**"All spirits who choose to have a life on Earth are
given a physical body in order to experience the physical
reality of the Earth plane. One day this body will die.
Be prepared, for this may come when you least expect it."**

"Ooooooh this is a spooky book, do you think we're gonna die today?" Brad asked.

"Maybe during the assessment," joked Matt.

"Yeah that'd be funny I can just see everyone's faces looking horrified as we keel over." Brad clutched his throat and pretended to fall.

"You've got a warped mind," Matt smiled. "You still having therapy?"

"Yeah yeah funny guy," he laughed pressing the button to call the lift to the express lobby.

8:00AM

American Airlines flight 11
leaves Logan Airport, Boston,
headed for Los Angeles.

8:01AM

One of my biggest fears about the day was for my widowed wife, Win. I knew she didn't take too well to grief. Who does? But she was still talking to me and holding on to me like I was only there yesterday and it had been twenty-one years since I'd died. Don't get me wrong this is quite sweet really and I still love her so much. I just want the best for her and I didn't know how she was going to take another death. Tuning in to her apartment I found Win shouting at the TV which was always one of her favourite pastimes.

"No! That's wrong missus," she yelled.

It used to drive me mad. Misty her new little poodle barked. This was her third, the others had died of various diseases and like me they were now in place of honour in the display cabinet. But I am pleased to say that I took pride of place in a beautiful wooden box and the dogs were in cardboard ones on a lower shelf.

"Even Misty knows that. Don't you Misty?" she continued.

"And the answer is…," the TV said.

"A quarter of a mile," she shouted.

"That is correct twin tower one stands at 1,368 feet tall and twin tower two stands at 1,362 feet which is approximately a quarter of a mile into the sky," the TV almost echoed.

"See we're too good. We should go on here," she said to Misty who wined and wagged her tail.

A well polished statue of Jesus beckoned Win's attention so she picked it up and started polishing it some more.

"Don't mind me Lord," she said softly. Win had taken the cleanliness is next to godliness too far as the house was always spotless. Some people would say she was obsessive but in the Catholic Church being obsessed with one's religion was not a bad thing.

She did amuse me most of the time but today I felt for her because it wasn't long before she'd be plunged into a state of grief again. As I transported myself into her flat Misty could sense me. Animals have very good psychic perception. Misty's was exceptional. She started sniffing so I put an energetic hand down to stroke her and she jumped back then sniffed it again.

"What you doing, Misty?" Win noticed.

The quiz show asked the question "In which tower of the World Trade Center would you find The Windows of the World Restaurant? Is it the north or the south?"

"North!" Win hollered totally oblivious to my presence in the room. "We went there once with Matt didn't we Misty?" she said, forgetting Misty didn't go because only guide dogs were allowed in and despite Misty's high intelligence she wasn't actually a guide dog.

"And the answer is correct, north..."

"When the Lord, our father was giving out brains I think he gave me and Misty a bit extra," she said talking at the statue she still had in her hand.

"And for a bonus point. How many floors are found in each of the twin towers, is it:

a)   150

b)   99

c)   110

"Oh that's a tough one," Win said. "Let's go for c."

Misty rolled over for me to tickle her tummy but just at that moment the phone rang which made her jump up with a start.

"Who's this at this time?" Win quizzed.

"Hi mom, it's Luke," he said over a crackly line.

"Hi Lukey," she said. "You're ringing early."

"And the answer is C, one hundred and ten," the TV said in the background.

"It's started," he informed, clutching his cell phone in the maternity ward of Lennox Hill hospital on the upper east side of Manhattan.

"Oh my…"

"Yeah, she's in the first stage now," he said sensibly.

"How's she doing?" Win asked.

"She's fine. But I know why they call it labour, its such hard work. I'm dead beat and I'm not even doing anything."

"Tell me about it, I've had four of the little rascals. It's like trying to squeeze a house out of your…"

"Mom, don't ruin it. I'm trying to make this a beautiful experience."

"I know I'm only teasing."

"Will you let Matt know?"

"I thought you'd fallen out."

"Yeah we have mom which is why I thought it'd be better coming from you. It's been a long time since New Year. I think we oughta just forgive and forget. You know move on. I wanna new start. I want this little one to know his uncle Matt. I just want it to be perfect. Maybe you could persuade him to call by the hospital mom, with Ro and the kids."

"I'll do my best honey but you know what he's like. There's no shiftin' him sometimes."

"Yeah I know. Thanks. I'll let you know when this little fella finally arrives."

The phone went dead.

"Another little soul you've sent to us, Jesus. You're so good to us," Win said as she put Jesus gently back in his rightful place next to me in the display cabinet.

8:14AM

United Airlines flight 175
leaves Logan Airport, Boston,
headed for Los Angeles.

8:16AM

Matt's 92nd floor open plan office was certainly a room with a view. It was a good job neither he, nor I, didn't mind heights. In fact, to Matt, being so high up with such a great outlook over the city was one of the perks of the job. Some days he'd just sit and stare through the window following the tiny, moving shapes down below him, as a way of switching off from the world.

Always on his arrival at work he'd sit, guzzling coffee to buzz him up for the day, while he checked his e-mails. Today was no exception.

Hey Matt. Thanks for a lovely evening. We had a ball. Let's do it again sometime. Rowena's a damn good cook. Hold on to that girl.

All the best

Kerry and John

P.S. You got yourself a gun yet after your run in with the New York street boys!?!

This reminded Matt of what had happened just a few months ago back in the summer.

It is late one night. Matt had left his office at 11:00pm and is making his way through the concourse towards the subway. There is nobody around when he hears a gun shot. It doesn't sound very far away.

Panicking, Matt decides not to hang around on the deserted platform and instead heads for the exit. It is unusually quiet and as he walks he hears footsteps quickening as though trying to catch him up.

"Run," I shout at Matt knowing he is in danger. Matt starts running.

Without spilling a drop Matt came out of his thoughts and put his coffee down on the desk whilst remaining transfixed on the computer screen in front of him. He continued scrolling through his e-mails avoiding the work-related ones and skipping to his friends and family.

And then shock horror! The words MOM NEW MAIL flashed across the screen and there was a message sitting in his in-box. Win had managed to work out how to do e-mails for the first time. Matt thought it was a miracle she had figured out how to switch the computer on, let alone how to do e-mails without me. So did I.

Dear Matt,

 Not seen you for a while son. Good job I got a photo.

Love you Mom xxxx

Although thrilled, feelings of guilt also began to surface about not ringing his mom enough. He felt even guiltier about Luke.

I was standing behind him projecting myself at around the age of forty because when I was on the Earth plane that was when I was in the best physical shape. But I knew in only a few hours I'd have to become a more recognisable figure.

"You should reply to that straight away son before you forget," I told him.

"I think I'd better reply to this straight away before I forget," Matt repeated to himself.

"And tell her that you love her," I added.

Matt signed off with his name and for a reason unbeknown to him felt compelled to put a 'P.S. I love you' at the end, which was very out of character so he soon hit the delete button as feelings of embarrassment took over.

One of Matt's male work colleagues came over to his desk.

"The boss just rang. He's not coming in 'til this afternoon, not feeling too good," he informed.

"What? What about the assessments?" Matt exclaimed.

"It ain't gonna happen 'til then if at all."

"Oh great!" Matt said, sarcastically and annoyed. "That puts my life on hold even longer."

"Don't shoot the messenger." Dave took a step back.

"It's just a pain in the ass. I wanted it to be all over today," Matt complained.

"Just chill out man, life's too short to be worrying about work."

Dave was right. And it was the second time he'd heard these words today. I had been trying to get that through to Matt for years but he was stuck in his own little prison of work, sleep, work, sleep. A victim of the dreaded rat race.

At the desk opposite a woman, who had never set foot in the office before, was looking through drawers, panicking slightly.

"Can I help?" Matt asked.

"Oh I'm sorry, you must be wondering who I am, some crazy lady throwing files around," she said extending her hand. "I'm Stuart's wife, Clare. Nice to meet you."

Matt had never met Stuart's wife in all the six years he'd known him. He had a rule about not mixing business and pleasure so it must be a serious problem for her to be up there on the 92nd floor of the south tower.

"I'm looking for insulin," she blurted. "He said he kept an emergency supply in his desk." She carried on searching, papers flying everywhere.

"I didn't even know he was diabetic," Matt confessed. One of Matt's downfalls was he didn't really take much interest in others. Although it was difficult for me to watch he had become more and more selfish as his life had progressed.

"He'll be fine, I'm sure," she said adamantly, trying to convince herself. "He's in the car park feeling really ill right now. His levels haven't dropped like this for years. But he'll be good. His number's not up yet. I'll make damn sure of that."

By now she had emptied the contents of Stuart's drawers all over the floor.

"Do you want someone to come down with you?" Matt questioned hoping she would say no, as he really didn't want to be inconvenienced.

"Oh its fine, it's all under...oh thank God there it is." She attempted a smile at Matt as she pulled the spare insulin out of the drawer. I smiled to myself knowing what Stuart's guide was doing. She was right. Stuart's number obviously wasn't up today.

In **The Earth Guide Book** it states:

> **"Spirit guides must not interfere unnecessarily in the lives of those walking the Earth, but are allowed to interfere when asked, and also when facing an emergency which could result in an Earth friend being harmed or leaving the Earth plane before their due time."**

"Thanks," Clare said as she dashed out of the office. Matt had not been very helpful really and wasn't about to be, by clearing up the papers she'd left everywhere. He'd had enough of other people's mess this morning. It would just have to wait. His thoughts were interrupted by the tune of "*Mission Impossible*" coming from the top of his trousers. Jake had changed his ring tone and Matt hadn't figured out how to change it back.

"Damn kids," he muttered to himself.

A few of the heads that had made it to work early, turned and smiled. His phone flashed up Rowena's name.

"Be nice," I impressed on him.

"Hi honey," he said, a little friendlier than earlier in the morning.

"Hi. I dunno how you managed this Matt but you forgot your briefcase with your assessment papers in."

"Jesus Christ, did I?" he shouted looking round his desk in a panic. "Oh no! Shit, I did! I told you my mind's been elsewhere recently."

"Shall I drop it by for you before I go to the library?" she asked, trying to make amends for what happened this morning, thinking it was her fault even though it wasn't.

I could hear Delilah in the background.

"Are you a crazy mama?" Delilah squealed. "Do you wanna get yourself killed? Do you realise I'm trying to save your ass by keeping you away from that damn building? When you ever gonna hear me?"

It is difficult for a guide sometimes to get the message through to their Earth friend, especially when they are not very receptive.

"No!" I shouted at Matt, trying to help.

"Thanks, that'd be great babe," he replied not listening to my guidance either. "Call me when you're in the building."

"Okay."

Delilah was going mad with Rowena for making such an offer. I knew this would ruin her plans to keep her away from the Trade Center. But on the Earth plane people have the will to do as they please. We, as guides, can use various methods to try and direct our Earth friends but at the end of the day it is still their choice. This is the challenge of free will.

8:17AM

"Hey where we going?" This was one of the passenger's thoughts on board flight 11 which I picked up as I transferred my awareness into the aircraft. The plane was starting to veer off its normal route and this customer obviously knew the flight path from Boston to Los Angeles well. It felt like he'd flown it a hundred times before.

In the cockpit the pilots had been rendered helpless so the hijackers could take control and divert the plane to New York, only a short flying time away from Boston. The group leader's energy field, or aura, was dull, grey and spiky. His eyes were shallow and glazed.

Also in the cockpit were ten spirit workers filling the small space with positive energy. The guides invisibly crowding the flight deck knew there was no point talking to the hijackers because nothing would get through. It was too late to divert this path. The point of no return had been crossed. According to **The Earth Guide Book:**

> **"Everything on the Earth plane is cause and effect. There is no set future but once a particular point is passed one possible future becomes a certain destiny."**

In this case the crash was destined.

In the sky, outside the Trade Center, I could see Doris who was now hovering in front of the 70,000 strong spiritual army poised on the edge of the Earth plane ready for action. She knew this was going to be a small operation in comparison to the others she'd been involved with, like The Witch Hunt, the Nazi concentration camps and more recently the African famines. But nonetheless it was still important. It didn't matter whether there were 10 million souls or whether there was just one. Each and every one was precious.

"All souls must come home," she instructed.

"Being suddenly flung out of your body in a major disaster like this is a shock especially when it is not expected," she said. "Remember, when they see you at first most souls will think they are hallucinating."

Her army were taking it all in.

"Be kind and be quick. We don't want any souls getting lost if we can help it."

A circle of light gathered around the two towers. Each one was being individually wrapped in a cocoon of spiralling, blinding, bright white light. The base of the north tower was totally immersed and the rest of the 1,368 feet of concrete was slowly disappearing into it.

Through the center of each tower were three stairwells A, B and C. Some of them would collapse or become impassable but others would remain intact. They were a central thoroughfare through which all spirits, dead or alive, would try to pass. So Doris had instructed that three strong beams of light fall through them. These beams would help boost the energy of those trying to escape and give guidance to those who had left their bodies, who were attempting to cross over. A group of angels built up the vibration, lifting it higher and higher and higher until both towers glowed brilliantly with light.

A golden pinnacle was set up as the main opening between the two worlds—the Earth plane and the spirit plane. This was the gateway most of the 2,800 souls, about to be killed, would use to get home.

As the creators of these luminous towers relaxed, Doris announced, "Earth rescuers to your positions now."

She commanded those assigned to go into the building and on to the streets to start their descent because within a few minutes the first signs of panic would be manifest. Flight 11 from Boston was on its way. I could see it approaching in the distance.

8:35AM

Further up Manhattan a bird's eye view over 7th Avenue saw a sea of moving yellow cabs. Matt and Rowena's 4x4 was one of the odd ones out as Rowena bravely faced the rush hour traffic to get to her husband.

"Calm down Delilah," I said as I teleported myself into the car. I knew I had to help Delilah stop Rowena from entering the building as there was a strong possibility that her entry would take Matt away from his desk, to a floor lower than the intended crash site. This could bring him a really sudden death, which in one way I wanted for him but on the down side wouldn't give him time to say his goodbyes.

Rowena was on her way back from dropping the children off at school and was listening to a self-help tape in the car as she drove through the madness.

The tape said, "Now repeat after me…I am confident, happy and strong. Life supports me in every way." Rowena more or less repeated, "I am strong, happy and confident and life supports me in every way…even if my husband is a workaholic who forgets his things and shouts at the kids."

"Good. Well done," said the tape.

"Thank you," replied Rowena. She continued in her own little world ignoring all messages that were coming her way from Delilah.

Delilah reached for her new copy of **The Earth Guide Book**, that she'd had to go back to the spirit world to get. She closed her eyes and opened the page. It read:

"On occasion a physical message is needed to keep your Earth friend on the right track."

Delilah knew exactly what she had to do and without hesitation lowered her vibration enough to have a physical effect on the radio-cassette player. She turned it off. As the tape suddenly stopped so did Rowena.

"Hey what happened?" she said, startled.

"I turned it off to grab your attention," Delilah told her.

Rowena turned it back on again and got a radio station. It was John Lennon singing "*Imagine*".

"Imagine all the people living for todaaaay," she sang.

Delilah turned it off again.

"You won't be living on this Earth at all, never mind today, if you don't listen to me honey."

"What's going on?" Rowena was confused.

She turned the sound system back on again.

"Good Morning New Yorkers. It's a beautiful sunny day in the city and I hope everyone is happy this morning. You're listening to 1010 and next we have a…"

Delilah turned it off again. The DJ's voice disappeared.

Rowena and Delilah were locked in a bizarre, half visible, competition to see who could keep the radio on or off and they repeated the exercise a few more times until eventually Delilah won.

It wasn't long before, amongst the noisy rush hour traffic, Rowena found herself with a flat tyre, which took an enormous amount of spiritual energy from both Delilah and myself to manifest.

The lamed vehicle was soon being slowly pushed off to the side of the road by a group of amenable men on their way to work. Angry motorists and dozens of cab drivers were beeping their horns with frustration but Rowena just ignored them. "I am happy, strong and confident," she repeated to herself as she floated towards the kerb, like a broken down old bumper-car, now only a couple of blocks away from Matt's office.

"You could probably leave it here now and get a tow truck to pick you up," one of the guys said through the rolled down window. "Dial 311 for the nearest operator."

"Yeah, thanks guys, so much," she said flirting slightly through the rear view mirror. "Hope you have a better morning than mine."

"No problem ma'am," a unison response came from the back of the 4x4.

The guy at the window hadn't left. "Sorry to bother you. I don't want you getting the wrong impression of me. I don't ask this question very often at all but I was wondering, you doin' anything special tonight?" he asked hopefully.

"Having dinner with my husband," she said holding up her wedding finger that was wrapped in a beautiful emerald studded ring.

"I hope he treats you well, you're a beautiful lady," replied the smooth talker. "If he doesn't here's my number." He handed her a card with the name of a very expensive 5th Avenue boutique on it and his name Mark Gibson.

"He does," she said refusing it and feeling sad because Matt didn't treat her well anymore. I wish I could have transported Matt's mind into Rowena's from time to time so he could see what she needed.

"I'm glad, you deserve it, but just in case he slips up, here." He threw his card onto the back seat of the car, smiled at Rowena and joined the others on their way back to work.

Rowena grabbed Matt's papers and got out of the car.

"Is she still going to the Trade Center?" I asked Delilah who knew her mind better than I did.

"That's what's in her head I'm afraid," was the reply.

We glided down Broadway. We didn't need to walk like people do because there was no need to. I quite liked hovering. It had taken me ages to master and was a really nice feeling.

Occasionally I nodded at some of the guides I saw in the streets. Normally I knew them because of the training I'd done in the spirit world. Sphere four is where all the training to do with the Earth plane takes place. I had completed the training ready for this day because I wanted to be the one who guided Matt back home. Ever since I left him on the Earth plane back in 1980 I had kinda felt responsible for the way his life took a dive. I now knew that I wasn't. Even **The Earth Guide Book** told me that. It said:

> **"Earth is a place of free will. People on Earth can even choose how they are going to react to anything that happens to them."**

"She won't get far in shoes like that, so don't worry. She could join the goddamn circus in those," Delilah said pointing at her pink stilettos.

Rowena suddenly stopped and bent over to attend to her shoes. They were starting to rub against the backs of her heels. She rested briefly before braving the rest of the journey.

A few more minutes of heel rubbing hell forced Rowena to the middle of the road to flag down a cab. This was going to pose more of a problem than she thought, however, as most taxi lights showed unavailable and were already full. After five minutes of trying she decided to walk. It wasn't that far now.

"I can't believe she's still walking!" I said.

"If there's one thing about my Rowena she's a determined lady," replied Delilah.

By the time Rowena arrived at the Trade Center the backs of her heels were pouring with blood. She didn't realise how bad they were until she put her hand down and turned her fingers red. She looked at them horrified, like she'd just committed a major crime.

Looking at the elevator doors she remembered last night's dream. The vivid images of the blood and the warning DON'T TAKE THE ELEVATOR that went along with it came back into her mind. But neither myself nor Delilah knew what Rowena would do. It was at times like these that we wished Earth wasn't a planet of free will. Would she ignore the warnings and take the elevator or would she take the stairs? This could turn out to be a life or death decision only she could make.

Rowena contemplated the stairwell for a few seconds but it wasn't a realistic plan. It would take hours to climb all that way and with her legs in such a state it wasn't really an option at all, dream or no dream, she thought to herself. So without further hesitation she walked into the elevator.

8:43AM

Matt was playing solitaire on his computer, trying to de-stress himself, when I arrived back with him. I put my hands on his shoulders and to my surprise he could feel it.

"Oh hi, I thought you were gonna ring me," he said thinking I was Rowena. "That's nice. Just give them a quick rub. Can you feel that knot? I'm so stressed out."

Obligingly I did. In all the years I had been doing this to Matt he had never once felt anything. I knew he was preparing to go and I wondered if he knew too.

"That's heaven," he said.

At this point the phone rang.

"Hello, Matt Moretti," he answered.

"Hi, it's me." It was Rowena's voice. "I'm in the building."

"What the…?" Matt yelled feeling completely freaked out as he swivelled his chair around fast, expecting to see someone else massaging his shoulders. There was nobody there, except me of course but he couldn't see me yet. I smiled at him.

"God I must be stressed. I'm even imagining things now."

"What you talking about?" She sounded puzzled.

"Oh nothing. It doesn't matter. I'll meet you in the sky lobby on 78, see you soon."

This meant Matt would not be at his desk on impact.

A loud humming noise in the distance interrupted his train of thought. His clock said 8:43am. The hijacked flight 11 to Los Angeles emerged from the horizon heading straight towards the city. Matt felt strangely constricted in his chest, a really weird feeling, like nothing he'd ever experienced before. His lost sixth sense was re-emerging and he knew something was wrong. But he had no idea this plane was going to crash into the north tower, next door, in a matter of minutes.

"What the hell?" he said to himself as he stood up. Picking up his jacket he headed for the elevator but was called back by his work phone.

"You'd better get that," I said to him.

He stopped for a split second and wondered if it may be Rowena again.

"You'd better get that," I said again.

He went back and picked it up.

"Hi Matt its Carla. I'm just ringing to say I'm gonna be late. For some strange reason my alarm didn't go off. I can't believe I've only just woken up," she panicked.

"Don't worry, Carla, he's not here," informed Matt.

"But what about the…?"

He interrupted. "Probably ain't gonna happen. So just chill Carla…Yeah I'm pissed too…Yeah I've been working on them all night too…no he doesn't care…I know…Yeah…ah ha…uh huh…yep…no I don't think so…aha…listen I've gotta go." If there had been an Olympic event for talking she could have represented America. Matt kept looking at his watch and was getting impatient with the call.

It was 8:45am.

"See you later," Matt finished, hanging up the phone and heading for the elevator for a second time.

There were now 10,000 angels in the buildings and on the ground. As they walked the Earth they raised the vibration of the area whilst waiting patiently for the inevitable.

Matt stood waiting for the elevator that would shuttle him down to the lobby, as the noise of the approaching plane got louder and louder until, suddenly, there was a colossal, ear splitting crash.

8:46AM

American Airlines flight 11
crashes into the north tower
of the World Trade Center.

8:46AM

The whole building shuddered, mimicking the effects of a mini earthquake. The sound of glass being shattered ricocheted off the surrounding buildings of the financial district and could be felt all the way up mid Manhattan to Central Park.

"What the hell was that?" Matt cried.

Even the guides were shaken, me included and we're not even physical. I dread to think what it must have been like for everyone in the north tower. Matt went back to his office window to have a look. All he could see was panic. Small figures, that looked ant like from Matt's high in the sky perspective, were darting around much faster than their usual rush hour pace.

He wished he had a pair of binoculars to enlarge the scene unfolding before him and thought back to the bombing back in 1993. Matt wondered whether they had managed it again. I remember having to keep him away from the towers on the day of the attack, but it was miniscule in comparison to today's mammoth events.

Looking down on ground level chaos had taken over. The plane had crashed like a rocket between the 94th and 98th floors of the north tower killing hundreds of people instantaneously. But Matt was unable to see the remains of the flying missile I could see and the gaping wound in the side of the north tower, as he was on the other side of the south tower.

Bits of debris from the building and the offices fell to the ground hitting passers-by, injuring some, killing others. People were screaming with fright, not knowing what was going on around them. Flames could be seen from below and tourists and citizens alike stood watching in horror. There was nothing anybody could really do until the emergency services got there and within seconds the alarms calling the fire-fighters were triggered and sirens soon screeched into downtown New York, Manhattan Island, the World Trade Center site.

This would be the biggest test the New York Fire Department had ever faced as the symbol of America's wealth and power was attacked. There was certainly never anything this epic in my day. It would only be another seventeen minutes before the south tower would fall prey to this brutal attack. But right now it was essential for both towers to be evacuated. Only a handful of people really knew that plus us, of course, the angelic rescue workers and helpers from the other side, who had foreseen the crashing of the two towers to the ground. This would happen within the hour and we were all fully aware. It was "all hands on deck" to calm those who were trapped, save those we could and help those that were already dead to pass over.

Doris would have long since sent her men and women down to ground level and the tunnel of light to the other side, I could see, was now more vivid than ever. Rescue workers were already helping people across, through to the next part of their lives into the spiritual world. To some there would be an initial shock and to others this would be the most comforting, liberating experience they had ever had.

It is hard for people to cross over when they are not expecting it. Imagine, one moment you're drinking your coffee checking your mail, the next instant you're decapitated by a chunk of steel in the back of your neck, all within a split second and you didn't even feel a thing. It's very disorientating, and as I keep saying that's not it when you die— you've got to then adjust to still being alive but suddenly you're without your body. Lying in a hospital bed, dying of cancer waiting for God

58

as your body gives up the fight is easier, as far as crossing over goes, because everyone, you included, is expecting death.

It wouldn't be long before not just a small handful of people knew about the disaster, because the TV news had arrived on the scene to broadcast live pictures to the nation, coverage which would also reach the rest of the world.

Matt knew Rowena was on her way and hoped she was okay. He reached for his phone and called her up.

Rowena answered and Matt quickly responded with, "Hi it's me. You alright?"

"No, not really, the elevator's stuck, something's happened, what's going on?"

"I think that was the north tower," Matt said. "A bomb or something maybe. It must have somehow affected the elevators in the south tower."

With my psychic eye I could see Rowena standing, barefoot, looking down at her feet trying to avoid all eye contact, whilst noticing her first-day-of-new-shoes nightmare with blood pouring off the backs of her heels. It reminded her of the dream again.

"Damn, I shouldn't be in here," she realised.

"No you shouldn't," agreed Delilah.

"What?" asked Matt.

"I had a dream last night about an elevator. It was gross. I shouldn't be in here. I know I shouldn't," she said panicking slightly and feeling annoyed with herself for not listening to her dreams.

"It was only a dream. It doesn't mean anything," Matt said. "You'll be out in no time. Just hang tight 'til they fix it."

Matt had no idea of the power of dreams and how they can be used to clear fears of the past, present and future, how they can be used as warnings and how they can be used to prophesise forthcoming events.

"At least we're not in World Trade Center one," she responded trying to be more positive in this potentially terrifying situation.

"Yeah thank God," Matt agreed.

A man in a suit with a very old, solemn looking face, who was on his way up to The Windows on the World Restaurant, for his breakfast, had turned a sickly green colour. He interrupted.

"I'm sorry. I wasn't meaning to listen in ma'am but this *is* number one tower."

"You're kidding?" Rowena said looking shocked.

Some of the others who were tapping away on their cell phones, also trying not to panic, nodded.

"Oh my God," Rowena cried. "Matt, I'm in the wrong building. I'm in the north tower."

8:52AM

"Jesus Christ Rowena, what you doing in there? You've gotta get out."

"How?"

I could see that out of the six others she was sharing her fate with, one of the other younger guys, who was on his way to The American Bureau of Shipping, on the 91st floor, had already taken it upon himself to use the emergency phone to contact the elevator operators. They were employed solely to look after the workings of the extremely important elevator system which was like the central cog that kept the building alive with workers.

What Matt and Rowena didn't know was that most of the attendants had already evacuated leaving a large number of people trapped between floors. They were relying on the emergency system, which had not long ago been installed for an event like this, that would trigger the elevators to automatically return to the bottom floor, opening their doors for passengers to escape.

In Rowena's situation the emergency system had not kicked in and they had just come to a halt between the 34th and 35th floors.

"Great, there's nobody answering," the guy informed.

"There's nobody answering emergency services. Can you ring them,

Matt, please?" she asked.

"What the hell are they doing?" Matt said crossly. "I'll see what I can do and call you back," Matt promised and hung up.

Matt rang down to the lift maintenance department and was assured by them that there would be people trying to sort the elevators out in tower one and not to worry because help would definitely be on the way.

"What's happened over there?" Matt investigated.

"We think a plane took a wrong route or was flying too low possibly and went straight into the side of the north tower," was the reply.

"Jesus!" Matt was speechless.

Matt tried ringing Rowena back but this time couldn't get through.

He picked up **The Earth Guide Book** that he'd put on his desk and opened it. It read:

> **"Make sure everybody you love knows
> you love them just in case you don't have time
> to tell them before you or they die."**

That was the third time this book had mentioned death and with Rowena trapped and the north tower fast becoming an all too real towering inferno he wondered whether he should start following the advice it was giving him.

He flicked it again and it said:

> **"Your universe sends you signs and messages.
> Take notice as they are there to guide you."**

He flicked it open one more time and it said:

> **"Freedom is a state of mind.
> You can be locked up and still be free."**

"What is this book?" he thought. I was pleased he had it with him.

Matt pondered its information further. "How can you be locked up and still be free?"

But Matt was thinking only of physical freedom. This statement was referring to the fact that we are at liberty to think whatever we want and from this comes great freedom.

"Do you think we need to evacuate?" asked Brad, as he found Matt trying unsuccessfully to contact Rowena again with **The Earth Guide Book** in his hand. The public address system of the building soon answered Brad's question. The announcement said:

"Your attention please, ladies and gentlemen. Building 2 is secure. There is no need to evacuate Building 2. If you are in the midst of evacuation, you may use the re-entry doors and the elevators to return to your office. Repeat, Building 2 is secure."

"You said that without moving your lips," Brad joked.

I knew the fire department would genuinely believe World Trade Center 2 was secure and would want to keep people away from all the burning metal, debris and now people falling out of Trade Center 1. They would think it safer to keep people inside.

Matt put the book down, looked up and said to Brad, "I think Rowena's gonna die."

"What you talking about Matt? You've been reading too much of that weird book."

"She's stuck in an elevator in the north tower," he replied.

"Oh jeeze! But don't worry, the attendants to those elevators are excellent. I'm sure she'll be out in no time," Brad said, ever the optimist.

"Are you on another planet Brad? A plane has just crashed into the building."

"A plane?"

"Yeah."

"How do you know it was a plane?"

"I just spoke to someone in the lobby."

Brad looked shocked.

"I'd better go see if I can help her," Matt said. I knew his worry for Rowena was in conflict with his own sense of being inconvenienced, as he rang her cell again without success.

"What's she doing in *there* anyway?" Brad asked.

"I forgot my assessment papers. She was bringing them in but she got the wrong building." Matt felt slightly embarrassed, then angry at her. "How could she get the wrong damn building anyway?"

"You must have done something good in a past life to end up with her," Brad interjected, trying to make light of the situation.

"I didn't think you believed in that weird stuff," Matt jibed, putting on his jacket as he prepared to leave.

"It can't just be bang and then it's all over. What'd be the point in that?" Brad defended himself as he followed Matt through the office.

"I think when you're dead, you're dead and that's it," Matt snapped pressing the button for the lift. He hadn't thought that when he was a little boy as he was highly religious, but my death had caused him to lose all faith.

"I hope you're wrong, buddy, but who knows. If you're not we'll meet up and have a beer in the next world eh," Brad said.

"Yeah, okay, you can pay for a change," Matt half joked.

Matt's cell rang. It was Rowena.

"Matt! What's happ…ing?" she cried over a broken line.

"I spoke to them. They reckon they've got guys working on it now but I'm on my way down now just to see what's going on," he replied. This was the first time in months Matt had said something reassuring to her. It had taken a traumatic situation like this for Rowena to realise that he might actually still love her.

"Freedom is a state of mind anyway," Matt repeated from **The Earth Guide Book**. Rowena was shocked at Matt's words. It sounded like something the Buddha might say.

"What?"

"I just read it in one of those books you keep by the bed," he said. "I don't believe it, but that's what it says."

It was slightly comforting to Rowena to hear his words partly because she was pleased he was reading one of her books but mainly, under the circumstances, she was more comforted to know the mechanics were working on the problem and help was on its way.

As the elevator door opened on Matt's floor he came face to face with his boss.

"Just leaving Matt? There's no need to evacuate. Didn't you hear the announcement?" he said in the sarcastic, aggressive tone he regularly used to intimidate people.

"I thought you weren't coming in," Matt defended.

"I never said that. I said I'd be late. I've managed to drag myself in to get these assessments done. I thought we'd start in say what..." He looked at his watch. It said 8:57am. "...fifteen minutes in the boardroom. You're up first." He walked passed Matt without even waiting for a response.

"My wife's stuck in an elevator in the north tower. I was just gonna check she was alright. Can we start a little later sir?" Matt said to his back.

"It's your choice Matt but if you're not there I'll just have to assume the pay rise you're after can wait another year," he replied without looking round.

He disappeared into his office.

"You bastard," Matt muttered under his breath.

Forgiveness was not an easy practice with this guy. Unfortunately I knew exactly what Matt was going to do. The same thing he'd been doing for the past ten years. If the boss says "jump" Matt says "how high?"

"I might have to stay with this loser," Matt said. Then suddenly he remembered, "But Rowena's got my assessment papers anyway! How can I do it without them?!"

"I'll go find Ro while you go talk to that idiot in there about your assessment, if you like," Brad offered. "Don't worry buddy. I'm sure she'll be fine."

My son looked at Brad while he weighed up the situation.

"Are you sure you don't mind?" Matt asked.

"Sure. No problem," he replied.

"Thanks Brad. I'll catch you up." Then remembering the message in the book he added, "But if for some reason I don't catch you up, when you find her tell her erm, well tell her, erm, tell her that I erm love her and I'll see her soon." His voice betrayed his embarrassment.

"You've been reading too much of that book. You'll be on Oprah next but I'll tell her," Brad jested, smiling at him.

8:56AM

It was unlikely Matt was going to find Rowena. Projecting my mind I could see her predicament still hadn't progressed. Rowena's elevator was capable of holding up to thirty people so it gave the seven of them in there, including her, a fair bit of breathing space and room to manoeuvre. Three of the guys, wearing the usual business attire, each with briefcases were speaking Japanese. Rowena thought this was a language that sounded far too fast and incredibly complex to understand. She wondered what they were talking about. One of them was carrying a set of golf clubs and seemed to be referring to them in his conversation.

"Typical men," Rowena thought, "stuck in an elevator that seems to be going nowhere and getting hotter by the minute and all they can talk about is golf." I couldn't help but smile at this.

Rowena was the only female in there. She slid down the side of the elevator wall. Her feet wouldn't hold her any longer. She couldn't believe the mess she was in. Nothing had gone right for her today but she told herself she wasn't going to panic. As her self-help guru from the tape kept saying in her head, "All is as it should be. You are in the right place at the right time. Your universe supports you in every way." She repeated this over and over to herself but was feeling incredibly skeptical. Delilah was working hard with Rowena's mind.

From outside the building I could see that the aircraft had impacted just as Doris had said, between the 94th and 98th floors, used as a weapon and deliberately tilted on an angle to cause even more damage. Stairwells A, B and C were being used by Doris and her team as tunnels to send light vibrations through to the escapees. The stairwells on the 92nd and 93rd floors were blocked tight on impact which meant anyone above them could not escape.

This was a fire fighter's nightmare. Any fire in the building was supposed to be contained on that floor so it could be fought by the fire crews while others could evacuate, but as I looked up at the mess I knew that this was one fire that wasn't going to be contained, as it raged through the north tower. People were coming to the windows crying for help and gasping for air. The fire officers put their efforts into evacuation and did the best job they could.

Fortunately Rowena was much lower than the impact site but nonetheless was in an elevator whose shaft could act as a bowling alley for fire balls thrown out from the crash at any moment.

Inside, the cabin was getting very hot. Rowena was doing her utmost to remain calm.

"Don't think the attendants are coming," said a young man wearing jeans and a cap who barely looked eighteen. He was a courier collecting a package from the 79th floor. "Maybe we should try force the door open."

"What floor we on?" another guy asked.

"I think we're stuck between 29 and 33. We're not that far up," said one of the Japanese contingent in flawless English.

"Maybe these'll help." He pulled out a golf club from a set of clubs he had with him by mistake. He was due to play at Chelsea Piers Golf Club after work but had actually got the day wrong. It wasn't until tomorrow evening. I knew this was not a mistake, however, and so did his guide.

"Fantastic, pass me a putter," said the elevator's head honcho. It doesn't take long to get the pecking order in place.

Two guys pulled either side of the door whilst another tried jamming in their new escape tool. A slight opening allowed him to wedge it diagonally and then pull it down until, suddenly, wham the doors snapped back to the closed position, the club fell to the ground and the lift dropped through the shaft like a torpedo. Stomachs flipped. Fear rose.

But unbeknown to them they had in fact triggered the safety mechanism which should have been activated when the plane impacted in the first place. It was programmed to return the elevator to the ground floor and open its doors. Much to everybody's relief this is exactly what it did.

They all charged out of the elevator into the lobby of the north tower, like it was release day, except Rowena who hobbled out holding her shoes by the straps. But the amount of debris on the floor meant she couldn't carry them for long as she would risk slivers of glass finding their way into her feet.

"Thank you. Thank you. Thank you God," she mumbled as she emerged from the cell-like structure.

The lobby looked like it had been set up as a command center. This wouldn't last long, however, as fire fighters themselves would soon need to be evacuated. Stuyvesant High School looked like the next probable location for the temporary operations center for rescue and recovery as I could sense the angels over there raising the energies. The school was now in the process of being evacuated, with kids being ferried across to New Jersey to escape whatever and whoever it was that was attacking New York.

Rowena was directed out of the area towards the underground concourse by a fireman and as she followed his instructions she told herself that she would never ever ignore her dreams again. Good idea, I thought.

9:00AM

Another distant humming noise was fast reaching a deafening and devastating crescendo. Flight 175 was on its way. Stuart's desk still stood empty as did quite a few others, vibrating slightly as the engines approached. I was starting to get nervous and was pacing up and down behind Matt, who had quite categorically been told by his boss not to leave the building and to continue his appraisals without his papers. Matt was fuming as he sat looking out of the window to the panic beneath him. He trusted Brad implicitly but would he be able to help Rowena?

I called on my inner strength to help us both get through this next bit as quickly as possible and I prayed for the best possible death for my son. I started to change my form, like a chameleon, to an older looking man, fifty-two to be exact, wearing the clothes of my passing, brown trousers and shirt to match. I wanted Matt to recognise me when he stepped out of the physical and onto the astral plane.

Matt turned to see the internal United Airlines flight heading straight towards the building.

"Oh my God. Not another one," Matt called out as he stood up. "This is turning into Pearl freakin' Harbour," he thought.

He was almost mesmerised by its surreal appearance out of the sky. Within a matter of seconds he watched it get closer and closer until it was so close he thought he could see the wide-eyed hijackers in the cockpit.

Matt screamed inside his head as it headed straight for the south tower. Terror gripped his body and mind in a rabbit-in-headlights moment, which felt like an eternity for both of us.

I saw Doris send a thousand rescue workers into the aircraft. They just seeped through the metal fuselage, osmosis like, vanishing into it.

9:02AM

United Airlines flight 175
crashes into the south tower
of the World Trade Center.

9:02AM

An invincible noise, of what felt like a hundred thousand panes of glass being shattered all at once, rushed through the building. It shook the astral plane too, and for a few minutes, as the airplane cut through its target, like a knife slicing a cake, everybody in the building was at the mercy of the attackers. Their location in the building at this precise moment would decide their destiny.

Some left their bodies instantly. Moments were lost to terror as people dived under tables, grabbed hold of one another or just prayed. Those on the 78th floor found themselves face to face with the light of the next world in an instant.

As everything settled down and the quake of the initial impact rumbled to its conclusion Matt looked himself over and realised he was, miraculously, still in one piece. All present and correct. Fortunately the plane had crashed several floors below and his office was not as directly in the flight path as he, or I, had originally thought.

The impact on the tower, however, had thrown him to the floor and he lay under a desk dripping in sweat, like he'd just done ten rounds with Mike Tyson, his shirt stuck to his skin. Frozen to the spot, too scared to move, he could hear screams and sounds of panic from both inside and, he thought, outside the building. I was trying to send him feelings of calm to melt the fear trapped in his body as he cowered like an animal, waiting and sensing his surroundings, wondering if it was safe to move.

A picture of Rowena flashed into his head. He knew that she was in the elevator in the north tower somewhere but didn't know exactly where, or if she was okay or if Brad had got to her. But there was no time to find out. Flames were licking up the side of the building and the heat was rising fast. Matt feared that if the heat rose high enough it would not only kill anyone in its reach but could also cause the steel structure, which holds one of the tallest buildings in the world together, to start to melt. This would be like melting someone's spinal column. The whole building, with him in it, could be reduced to a pile of rubble within minutes. He hoped the designers of the building had planned for every eventuality.

I knew a core collapse was a serious possibility as the extra jet fuel on board the planes would, without doubt, raise the temperatures to astronomical levels.

Matt knew he had to work fast to beat the smoke and the heat. He was just glad his office wasn't a few floors below. He tore off his shirt, with no concern for his growing beer gut and made his way to the stairwell. There were a number of people trying to get down but the smoke was rising fast. Using his shirt as a mask to block the fumes he started the descent into the unknown, hoping and praying there was a way out. As he went further his eyes started smarting and the smouldering heat made him feel odd and sick.

"This is suicide," he thought, as he continued through it anyway. "What should I do? Carry on? Find another way down? Go to the roof? Wait to be rescued?" His mind was racing and was far too busy for any of my suggestions to get through. It was only made up when he heard Brad's familiar voice, not quite as jovial as it had been only a few hours ago, saying,

"Turn back, turn back, it's too much down here. We'll have to try another stairwell."

"Brad is that you?" Matt yelled.

"Matt?" a dim voice projected.

"Yeah it's me Matt."

"Turn back Matt it's impossible down here," Brad cried.

"Are you sure?"

"Hundred per cent sure!"

"Did you find Rowena buddy?" Matt shouted. There was a long pause and no reply.

"Did you find Rowena?" he repeated but again with no response from Brad. "I'm gonna head for the roof, I'll see you up there."

Brad didn't engage as he was using all his energy to escape the grip of the rising heat and the strange smelling smoke.

Brad had managed to get to the bottom of the tower to try and find Rowena but wasn't allowed to cross the normal route to WTC1. He was firmly instructed by the fire department that it was all under control and he would only be a hindrance, not a help, if he tried to go into WTC1. He was reassured that they would try and find Rowena and free everyone in the elevators. Brad was on his way back up and stopped at the 92nd floor when the plane hit the building. He leapt out of the elevator seconds before it disappeared, falling through the building like a dropping bomb, after its cables were severed by the crash.

Matt headed back up towards the roof with me behind. He was convinced that once up there the New York emergency services would be airlifting people to safety. What he didn't know was that a decision had been made not to send in the rescue choppers—it was far too big a risk as the smoke and fire could block the pilots' vision causing further problems.

Nobody really knew what was going to happen next either. Another plane might be on its way. Evacuating the north and south tower by foot seemed the most obvious solution.

"It'll be cooler on the roof, I'll see you up there man," Matt shouted down to Brad but there was still no response. He saw Rowena in his mind's eye again and for a moment realised how much he really depended on her. The thought of never seeing her again filled him with dread. As he climbed up the stairs his mind started to flashback to the night they first met.

He remembered how gorgeous she looked with her long black, curly hair, flicked behind her bare back and the skimpy tight, black dress she was wearing, at an office bash at the Plaza Hotel on the corner of 5th. Then a year later, by some strange coincidence they bumped into each other again, during the interval at a concert in Carnegie Hall. Rowena figured there was no such thing as a coincidence and asked him whether he thought it was a sign that they were destined to be together. To which his reply was "yes" even though he didn't believe in signs or any of that esoteric nonsense.

But now the thought of her being trapped in that elevator and the possibility of not seeing her again didn't bear thinking about. He had a flicker of regret about some of the things he'd done in the last few years, things he hadn't allowed himself to think about too much because they would have weighed too heavily on his conscience. He couldn't fully go there yet but he vowed he would make it up to her when they got out of this crazy situation.

A big, big guy, who'd eaten one too many pizzas, who was heading down the stairs shoved passed him jolting Matt out of his reverie and back to the reality of the building.

"Hey watch it…there's no way down that way," Matt shouted at him. But he just ignored his warnings and carried on going on automatic pilot, soon to meet the same impenetrable obstacle Matt had.

Tuning in to several floors below us, where the hijackers had chosen their grisly terminus, I saw people who had been shocked out of their bodies a millisecond before the plane nosedived through their offices and into the elevator lobby. There were hundreds of light workers standing, like warriors, ready to dissolve the fear the terrorists were creating. Help was there for all these people as they left their bodies, even the terrorists themselves. It sometimes takes a while for the newly dead to register that indeed that is what they are. Nobody has ever taught us or shown us what happens on death. It wasn't on the school curriculum.

The guiding lights stood shining through the smoke, licked by flames which could not touch their immortal presence. They pulled people, now in astral form, towards the next realm of vibration, into the light. It was a seductive feeling of peace that drew them closer.

Golden spirals of light swirled everywhere. These were the tunnels, or gateways, that joined with the giant vortex at the peak of the twin towers. Outside, on this beautiful sunny morning of Tuesday September 11th 2001, the towering vortexes, which existed only in this bridging dimension of life, were spinning faster than ever as souls fled from the building into the safety of their homecoming energy.

Matt now climbing the stairs to the roof was getting frustrated by the slow pace.

"What's the damn problem up there?" he shouted. "Come on, let's move it, we ain't got all day," he yelled.

There were also people trying to make their way down. He just let them go by. There was no point trying to stop them. A woman in her fifties collapsed on Matt in exhaustion. Her thickly plastered make-up had started to run like a plastic doll-face melting in the heat.

"What you doing?" he snarled at her.

"I can't go any further," she whimpered.

"Yes you can, come on get up," Matt said lifting her up. But like a bar-bell too heavy for him, gravity and exhaustion took over and he let her fall to the floor.

Her friend, following her down, turned on Matt. "You can't just leave her there," she snapped, telling him off as though he was twelve. Matt was fraying at the edges. This was not the kind of day he had envisaged. He'd rather be doing his assessments.

"You carry her then," he snapped back.

"You call yourself a man?" she said trying to change his mind.

"Not today. No, not today lady I'm not," he said pushing forward.

"So are you just going to leave her there?"

Matt looked down at the woman lying in a heap, who looked like she was about to faint.

"We have no choice! It's impossible to carry her," he said and carried on up the stairs.

"You asshole!"

Unusually for Matt he just let this go. Under normal circumstances he would have argued to the bitter end, until he had asserted his authority. But I knew he had as much intention of getting into a fight now as he did of picking this woman up off the stairs.

"She'll die if we leave her here," she screeched.

"We'll all die if we try and help her," Matt yelled back.

The fact was that they were all destined to leave the Earth plane whatever they did now. The point of no return had been crossed. The real tragedy for Matt was that he did not try and help. He selfishly soldiered on upwards thinking only of himself. I knew he would regret that later when he crossed over.

Matt felt like he'd just been teleported through the TV screen and onto the set of *The Towering Inferno*—a film he'd watched a dozen times or more, over as many Christmas seasons. He wished it was so. He wished he was at home.

His thoughts drifted back to the New Year. It was like his mind was trying to take him somewhere else to avoid what was really going on.

"...Can I have your attention please, I'd just like to make an announcement that something amazing is gonna happen to our family next September. Go on Lorraine you tell them," Luke says, standing on his feet with a glass of wine in his hand. "Fill your glasses everyone." Everyone obeys the instruction. "Go on Lorraine tell them."

There is a long pause before Lorraine beams at her adopted family the words, "I'm pregnant."

There is a raucous cheer.

"Aw congratulations honey, I'm so thrilled," Win squeals, leaning across the table to hug her.

After the excitement calms down Luke turns to his younger brother and says, "So Matt, how's it going at work?"

"Fine," Matt replies not really engaging in conversation much. He is slowly getting himself very drunk.

"Luke's been asked to handle a new young band for one of the major labels. Haven't you Luke?" Lorraine says a little competitively.

This really riled Matt.

Music used to be his one and only love until I died back in 1980 and then he kinda lost interest in life, didn't take the opportunities that were presented to him and found himself getting into financial markets and a career that, although he was good at, didn't make his spirit sing. This was not his life's work.

"Oooooooo lucky Luke, new young band for one of the major labels," Matt says mimicking Lorraine and being deliberately offensive.

"Matt!" Rowena says.

"Are you drunk Matt?" Luke shouts.

"Well, I'm sick of it. New job, new band, new car, new house, new baby, always thinking you can get one over on me with that smug little face," Matt pushes his chair back to leave. "I can't eat with him."

"Matt?" Rowena says.

"Grow up Matt," grates Luke.

"Grow up yourself. You're not dad, you know," Matt says.

"Don't bring dad into it!" Luke responds getting angrier by the second.

"Don't tell me what to do. You always think you can tell me what to do. You

think you're so freakin' good."

"No I don't. Matt what's gotten into you?"

"He's stressed at work. I'm sorry for his behaviour," Rowena says.

"No I'm not. Work is just fine. In fact it's great," he lies, as he is close to losing it at work.

"If you're gonna be like this I think you should leave," Luke tells him.

"Don't worry that's exactly what I'm gonna do," Matt snarls as he leaves the room. A few seconds later he slams the front door, rocking the whole house with his anger.

He'd felt bad for weeks after that event, especially after they'd announced they were having their first baby. So it didn't surprise me that it surfaced now because he hadn't dealt with it yet. He didn't really understand what came over him that day but his behaviour had been getting more and more erratic as the months went by, coinciding with the fact that he was given more and more responsibility at work.

Deep down Matt was a very sensitive guy and pressures on him really took their toll on his nerves. And like many people on the Earth plane they take out their stress on those they love the most. To me it seems to be a bizarre part of the human experience, but **The Earth Guide Book** says:

> **"On Earth people either behave with lower instincts and intentions or with higher ones. Striving towards a higher state of being is much preferable for the vibration of the individual and the planet."**

Matt arrived at the floor below the roof where he found some people hanging out up there, just waiting. They were trying not to panic, though without the least hope of success. As far as they were concerned New York was under attack and their building was in the direct line of fire. Cell phones were ringing. People were terrified. A group of young accountants were trying to have a calming effect by telling everyone that it would be just fine. But Matt wasn't listening to them. He waited at the top of the stairs for Brad.

Brad had been drawn in to the crisis of the fainting woman on the stairs who'd begged and sobbed for him to help. He did try but didn't really get very far. As a result the two women's bodies lay dead on the stairwell and so too did Brad's.

Matt assumed Brad had found another way down or changed his mind about the roof.

The exit door to the roof was locked.

"Damn I'm a prisoner," he said, as he rattled the door.

Matt wasn't the first to try it. Even though others warned him there was no escape that way, he just had to check for himself.

He remembered **The Earth Guide Book** and the statement about being free even if you're locked up. It still didn't make any sense to him. He slapped his hand on his backside to feel his pocket. The book was still sticking out of it. Somehow he'd formed an attachment to this manuscript and it had become a kind of ally to him, even though he didn't believe in it. Subconsciously it also made him feel closer to Rowena.

The smoke signals of distress, from the lower floors, billowed upwards. Matt didn't know what to do next. Looking over the side of the building through a broken window on the 109th floor, he could now observe WTC1 where he saw more orange flames in offices below, and more smoke. People were hanging out of windows crying for help, desperate to get away from the heat and the writhing white smoke leaking from the building, which was obviously consuming their world. Some looked like they were preparing to jump.

Matt also thought about it and wondered whether by some act of God he might jump and miraculously survive the impact. But he didn't believe in God, nor was he stupid enough to think wishing could suspend the laws of physics. His only hope was that the firemen would put out the blaze, clear the stairwell and come and save him. For a moment he felt glad he paid his taxes.

The other option, of being airlifted to safety, which he'd thought might be his best chance, was failing fast. There was no sign of that happening. Not a helicopter in sight.

"It ain't looking good is it?" a guy from Euro Brokers said, who should have been on the 84th floor, but was on his way up to meet a colleague on a higher level, when flight 175 hit. He too was leaning out of the window.

"My wife's probably in that building too," Matt said feeling resigned to watching it burn like some kind of bad dream.

The Earth Guide Book says:

> **"Life is a dream but it's only the moment you
> wake up that you realise you've been dreaming."**

"No shit. It's double jeopardy for you today. I'm sorry man," he said.

"Got a plan then?" Matt asked him.

"Just sit tight and wait for the fire fighters, I suppose or build a hang-glider or extra long rope or parachute or something like that. Shit knows," he replied. "The smoke and heat's gonna bust us soon."

Ironically Matt was desperate for a cigarette. The craving was now greater than ever but he didn't have any. The kind of toxic smoke that was coming from the south tower could probably kill a healthy lunged man within minutes, he guessed. He didn't want to start compromising his lungs at this stage though. He wanted to keep his chances of survival as high as possible and wished he'd given up smoking years ago. But the craving was too urgent for him to resist. The thoughts of a relaxing *Marlboro* moment, taking away all the stress, entered his brain and body and, like any addict, he had to have a cigarette and he had to have one now.

"Do you smoke?" he asked his new friend.

"Are you kidding?" the guy snorted.

A friend no more. I didn't think Matt would stop here for his fix, and was proved right as he started pestering other people, who were either

82

on the phone trying to find out what to do next or trying to contact their friends and family. Most were totally unsympathetic but eventually he found a young woman on her own in a corner, smoking and sobbing at the same time.

"You got any cigarettes left?"

She looked up at him through her bloodshot, tear filled eyes and just stared at him. She said nothing.

"Can I buy one off you?" Matt grovelled.

Eventually she reached into her handbag and slowly retrieved a packet. They weren't his brand but he didn't care. She flipped open the box and pulled one out.

"I'll swap it if I can use your phone," she whispered.

Matt knew he didn't have much battery left but would have swapped his left leg for just a drag at this point.

"Sounds like a deal to me," he said, as he reached into his pocket and handed her his tiny, Japanese made, cell phone.

She paid her dues and Matt lit up his cigarette with her lighter, taking a deep inhalation of smoke, which caused him to splutter slightly. "That's good," he thought as he inhaled. He couldn't help but overhear her conversation.

"Hi mom it's me. I'm sorry you're not there but listen I just wanted to tell you that I love you so much and thank you for being such a fantastic mom. You're one in a million mom and I love you so much…" She started sobbing again. "I can't promise I'm gonna get out of this building…I'm almost on the roof of the south tower and we're all waiting to be rescued, but if I don't make it then look after Bess for me please…She's not very demanding but she does need to go out twice a day. And look after yourself, and tell everyone that I love them, and don't spend a fortune on the funeral. It's not worth it cos I won't be there to appreciate it. But if there is life after death, like you always say, then I'll find a way to come back to you and let you know…I love you so much mom…" She sobs again then hands the phone back to Matt without switching it off.

Her guide, a young girl, of about the same age, is standing beside her. "You'll talk to her again," she said, but only her subconscious mind heard it.

"Thanks," Matt said, a little disturbed by her message, hoping she was just being over dramatic and they would be rescued very shortly. I knew he hadn't given up on the fire service yet.

"Call Rowena," I urged, wanting him to make contact soon.

Obediently he finished his cigarette and tried ringing Rowena again. If she was still alive, which he was sure she was, she'd be worried sick about him. He was cursing himself for licking his boss's ass and putting his job before his wife, which he realised he'd been doing for years. He also realised, which felt like a slam to the solar plexus, how much he really loved Rowena. A third realisation made him see that he didn't show it. "Love is action," he thought to himself. "Where the hell did that thought come from?" I smiled to myself.

Matt could not make a connection to Rowena, nor could he stay where he was any longer. He thought his next plan should be to find a room somewhere in the building, preferably close to the roof and lock himself in it until the fire had been dealt with and then just wait for the rescue. But he wasn't sure. His desperation forced him to reach to his back pocket and pull out **The Earth Guide Book**, which on opening said:

"Retreat – time on your own can bring about great healing."

"It kinda fits," he thought which gave him the extra kick he needed to make the journey into the building to search for this new healing place.

9:15AM

But where was Rowena now? I had to find out. Thinking of her and Delilah I found myself in the ladies' rest room of the south tower. She had obviously still been on her briefcase mission, when the second crash happened. On impact she had been flung backwards from the ladies' mirror into one of the cubicles behind her where she landed on the toilet, a seat I was sure she desperately needed by now.

"Hi, how you doin'?" Delilah greeted me, as she sensed me entering her arena. "How's Matt? He crossed yet?"

"No, not yet. He's a way to go."

"How about Ro? How's the mission?"

"She's so stubborn. Praise the Lord I gave her that dream though. She'd have been in another elevator on her way up to two floors down from heaven when that second one hit, if it hadn't been for that goddamn dream," Delilah replied.

But right now Rowena was in shock and still battling with her shoes. The pain was so excruciating when she tried putting them back on that she threw them across the room and they bounced off the condom machine onto the floor. Her tights were the next to go. She whisked them off, launching them towards the trash can but her token effort lacked force and they landed a few feet in front of her.

In her mind she was trying to figure out what on Earth was going on. It was not until a woman, clutching her crotch to avert a very embarrassing accident, came rushing in, to use the toilets, that she found out. She passed Rowena's open door and almost fell into the next cubicle down.

"Aaaaaah, thank God, for that!" The woman voiced her relief. Rowena, Delilah and I couldn't help but listen to the trickling as it hit the sides of the toilet bowl.

"Ask her what's happening?" Delilah prompted Rowena.

"I'm sorry to interrupt but do you know what's going on?" Rowena asked.

"She got that one," Delilah said surprised that her Earth friend took any notice.

There was silence for a while as Rowena's neighbour came to terms with the fact that someone else was using the rest room and had just asked her a question. Once she realised it was aimed at her, her reply was as appalling as it was prompt.

"There's been another crash," this new voice echoed round the rest room.

"What?" exclaimed Rowena.

"A crash. You know, two things colliding together."

"Did something hit the building?"

"You got it lady. A crash."

"What hit the building?"

"An airplane."

"Oh my God. A plane hit the building?" Rowena couldn't believe it.

"Yeah. I feel sorry for those poor people above us. They're most likely dead. We'd better get out quick before there's a third. It's probably the Russians," she panicked.

"What floor, do you know?" Rowena asked.

But it was too late to get a reply to that. This newcomer wasn't hanging around. She flew passed the cubicles buttoning up her trousers as she went.

Clutching her cell Rowena willed Matt to ring her. "Matt where are you?" she implored on the edge of tears. She now knew he could well be dead which would explain why he wasn't answering his phone. She tried again.

"Answer the goddamn phone Matt," she demanded.

She got through to his voice mail.

"Hi this is Matt. I'm sorry I can't talk to you in person. Please leave me a message and I'll call you back when I can...*beep*"

"Matt, where are you honey? Are you alright? I'm in the rest room in the south tower now. I'm fine. Are you alright, baby? Call me as soon as you can babe. Please call me," she rambled desperately.

Rowena was beaten every time by the voice mail. She wanted Matt. She needed him. Where was he?

Barefooted and barelegged she rose from her seat with a look of determination that had Delilah worried about her next move. Was Rowena mentally preparing to take on the blaze of the World Trade Center to find Matt?

9:20AM

Matt was wandering around, like an animal looking for a hideaway, along the deserted corridors of a lower floor, when my consciousness arrived back with him. He was trying doors which appeared to be locked. I could feel the frustration and the fear rising within him. He tried one final door. Miraculously it opened. This was going to be his retreat.

It was some kind of store room with boxes of stationery stacked up against the walls. He also spotted boxes of confectionery. "Good. Rations," he thought. "This will do."

Then SLAM. The door was shut. He enjoyed a moment of temporary relief to be away from the drama and shut in a room of his own choosing, not dictated to by suicidal pilots. He decided to use the boxes to barricade the door to stop any lung-hungry smoke from crawling under the door frame. He dragged them across the room and started piling them against the door. A box of chocolate bars, he put to one side for later, and another box of soft drinks he thought may come in useful, as he could be there for hours, he thought. He had no idea that in less than forty five minutes the south tower would fall.

After taking a few swigs of the diet Pepsi he decided it was a good idea to throw it over the cardboard boxes to prevent them from catching fire and it wasn't long before his barricade was a fizzing, wet mess.

Sweat was pouring off Matt as he worked, and for every minute that went by the temperature seemed to rise further and further. He stripped down to the Calvin Kleins Rowena had given him for Christmas last year, making a cushion for himself with his shirt and trousers. Looking at the red hearts on his boxers made him yearn for her, which was a feeling he hadn't had for years.

9:21AM

Bridges and tunnels leading
into Manhattan are closed.

9:24AM

Rowena was swimming up the stairwell, like a fish against the tide, thinking of nothing else but Matt. Delilah was sending me these images to let me know what was going on and asking for extra help.

Voices with no heads kept telling her to turn back, that the building was being evacuated and she was putting herself in jeopardy. But she blanked their suggestions. Nothing could deter her. She wasn't thinking logically. Delilah was at the end of her tether wondering "what on Earth" to do next.

Reaching for her guide book, she needed an answer. She opened it and the page read:

"Praying for divine intervention is always an option."

Despite having had a problem with religion and the concept of God in her past life, Delilah did not have a problem with divine intervention. And since she had died and spent time in the spirit world, she knew now that she did indeed, have a maker. A divine energy of love, was how she viewed "God", and this was who or what she was going to pray to.

"Please God, love, divine energy, the highest state of being, whatever you are, please help me. Rowena needs to be stopped right now. She is heading up the building towards an untimely death. Please help. Please."

Within a split second of this request Rowena was intercepted by a very handsome, very sweaty, unusually calm fireman who, in his full protective gear, had climbed, not far behind Rowena, up the staircase. His journey from the first call back at the station had been one of both excitement and fear. I remembered that feeling well from my days on Earth. It was a buzz a lot of the boys joined the fire department for. Catching sight of Rowena heading up, not down, carrying her shoes, he interpreted as a civilian disobeying orders, putting herself and possibly others in jeopardy. His job was to save lives and here was one he could save. He pushed himself harder and faster to catch her up, and as he closed the gap, put his hand out and firmly gripped Matt's courageous wife on the shoulder, like a parent would with a young child hell bent on dangerous mischief.

"Ma'am, I'm sorry but you can't continue up the building."

Rowena spun her head round to see his concerned eyes meeting hers, connecting with her spirit. On an astral level I could see their auras merging briefly. This merging of auras happens when you look into the eyes of another. This is why sometimes it is difficult to look someone in the eye as your energies merge. For a split second, Rowena felt better for his loving calmness and he felt worse because of her panic and fear.

"But...my...husband...is up there," she said between breaths.

"I will try and find him ma'am," he replied reassuring her. "You have to evacuate."

"I can't leave him," Rowena cried, causing her make-up to run further down her black-streaked face. "I can't leave him," she said again, holding on to the fireman.

"You have no choice ma'am. I have authority over this building now and you must evacuate. You cannot go any further."

"But..."

"You will die up there," he said firmly.

"Does that mean my husband will die?" she sobbed.

"The sooner you turn around and start heading for the exit ma'am the sooner I can go up there and try and find him."

After a short pause she said, "His name is Matt Moretti. He works on the 92nd floor, he's 32, about 6' 2", Italian looking, you know dark wavy hair…"

"Okay ma'am. I'll do my best. Now please go."

Turning her back on the fireman was like turning her back on Matt. It made her feel like she was abandoning him. She felt totally out of control but followed his instructions, nonetheless, making her way back down the crowded stairwell. People were descending at quite a steady pace, reacting in their own different ways—some crying, some focused, some calm, some panicking inside. But surprisingly most people were calm. Everyone was locked up in their own thoughts and survival instincts were running high. Stay quiet, conserve energy, don't alert the enemy of your whereabouts. Rowena fell in line and was soon washed away in a sea of Trade Center workers.

9:26AM

All domestic flights are grounded by US Federal Aviation Administration.

9:27AM

Back in his little hideaway Matt's body was exhausted. A restless night's sleep didn't help prepare him for the day ahead. In fact nothing could really prepare him. I think even my thoughts and efforts toward him must have had minimal impact. Adrenalin had kicked in some time ago and his system was living on fear. He was trying to be as normal as he could in this very abnormal predicament. It's not everyday a plane crashes into the side of your office building.

Matt sat down on the floor crossed legged and admired his modern art creation around the door frame. Wondering what Rowena would do in this situation, he wished he was with her. He didn't wish her to be trapped with him, of course, but she was very good in a crisis. Remembering a night on the way back to New York, from a holiday in Vermont when the brakes in the car suddenly went, Matt's mind recalled the events:

"I can't see a goddamn thing here," Matt says, leaning forward to get closer to the road, windshield wipers on full speed. The rain is bouncing off the glass like pellets.

"Just slow down as much as you can and stay calm," Rowena says leaning back in her seat.

It is really difficult to see. Then as he puts his foot down on the brake there's no resistance. It goes straight to the floor.

"Oh shit," he says alarmed.

"What's up?" Rowena asks.

"The brake. The brake's gone," he says repeatedly banging his foot to the floor.

"Just stay calm," Rowena says. "Stay calm."

"Rowena where are you?" Matt said out loud.

Matt then remembered another time when three-year-old Jake went missing on the biscuit aisle on a very, very crowded Thanksgiving eve in their local supermarket. She didn't yell. She didn't scream his name. She very methodically found him. First she went to customer services where they put an announcement out, then up and down each aisle, one by one, until she discovered him hiding on a low down shelf, behind the cornflakes, playing with a free plastic action model from one of the packets.

But where was Rowena right now? How was she coping with this? This was a real test. Matt wondered whether his phone was working. He grabbed it from his belt and saw he had missed messages. Listening to Rowena's voice was comforting. At least she was safe. It was now she who was worried about him. He blamed it all on his boss, not taking any responsibility for his actions. I wish he could realise that you are responsible for all your actions. If you blame someone else for them then you are giving your power away and losing control of your life.

He tried Rowena again. Clutching her phone, like a lifeline to her husband, she answered with desperation in her voice.

"Matt!"

"Yeah it's me. You alright?"

"Thank God. I thought you were dead!" she said not answering his question.

"Where are you?" Matt asked.

"I'm heading through the concourse," she replied.

Most of the evacuations were taking place through the underground shopping mall and concourse that connected up with the subway system. This was the safest way for people to leave the area, avoiding falling debris from the two buildings. Rowena was on her way through and was surprised her phone actually worked. Maybe it was some kind of divine intervention, she thought.

Doris had estimated at the meeting that 14,000 people would be in the two towers at the time of the disaster. A large number of them were now surrounding Rowena on all sides. A flood of people walked quite briskly and calmly out of the center. I sensed most of them were contemplating their lives up to this point and praying they would be able to carry on with them. Facing death or seeing someone die or a near death experience changes your perception of life. It makes you realise your own mortality.

Most people spend little if any of their lives monitoring or changing their thought patterns in their normal everyday lives. Now, in a crisis, many minds raced uncontrollably with fear. Your thoughts and past experiences create your world, every single one of them.

**"Mastering the thoughts of the mind in this lifetime is
a very good idea in order to achieve happiness."
(The Earth Guide Book)**

"Get as far away from here as possible. We just don't know what's going to happen next," Matt yelled.

"Where are you? Please tell me you're on your way out," she yelled back.

"No, I'm trapped," he replied.

"This is a nightmare. You've gotta get out Matt," she pleaded as the tables were now turned.

"I can't get passed the fire. It's too hot to go any further down and the stairwells are blocked," he said, sounding quite calm considering his circumstances.

"Matt, I couldn't bear it if anything happened to you, I love you."

"Tell her you love her, Matt, quickly," I urged him.

These were the words she wanted to hear from him but he never delivered. A faulty operating system in Matt's head—normally too jam packed with more important things like stats and equations.

The phone crackled making the reception unclear.

"I think I'm gonna lose you," she said, not knowing how close she was to the truth.

Rowena was spewed out of the concourse on to Liberty Street with a handful of other people. Outside chaos reigned. There were bits of ash floating around. Sparks were tumbling downwards. People were shouting. Some were running away from the building fleeing in all directions to safety.

Rowena looked up at the north tower and could see straight into the enormous hole which raged with smoke and fire.

Matt could hear that Rowena was now outside, as the tone had changed and the noises coming through her cell phone were different. She started running with the crowds towards Brooklyn Bridge.

"Ro, Ro!" Matt shouted at the phone. "Ro, Ro, Ro I love you. I love you, I love you," he said but she couldn't hear him. There was too much going on around. He thought he heard her say the words, "Oh my God" but couldn't be sure.

Rowena's attention had been captivated by a man high up near the crash site who was climbing through a window. He looked like he was about to take his own life by throwing himself from the tower. He had decided to take control of his own fate and this man-made furnace was not going to be his final destroyer.

On the astral plane, angels were flying around America's burning financial pillars waiting for people to jump.

"Oh my God," Rowena exclaimed, as did quite a few others as he plunged to his death. His body dropped, lead like, to the ground much to the horror of those watching. Rowena gasped, as did the world through the eyes of CNN.

Then nothing. The phone cut off.

"I'll get this soul," Doris shouted, as she swooped behind the brave man, to catch his astral body, as he left his physical form a split second before it hit the ground. This is a built-in mechanism in all of us where the instant before death the spirit moves out of its body to avoid any unnecessary pain or discomfort.

"Are you alright?" she said as she held him in her arms whilst heading towards the light, like a scene from *Superman*.

"Yeah, I think so," he replied. "Am I dreamin'?"

"No you've just left your body and you're on your way home," she smiled at him. "Earth is only a temporary home."

Rowena was frantically trying to reconnect to Matt but they were no longer on the same frequency. She couldn't get a signal. She'd lost him.

9:30AM

As the rescue continued on the Earth plane the spirit rescue continued on the next plane. Matt plucked **The Earth Guide Book** from his back pocket opening it for some reassurance. I knew the right message would come to him.

It said:

**"Live your life in a state of completion.
It will make dying much easier."**

For some reason he knew this was right. His life flashed before him. It was no way in a state of completion but how could he complete it now? He was stuck on the 105th floor of the south tower in an inferno, possibly about to die. What on Earth could he do?

"Use your phone again," I said. They may frazzle your ears and destroy the electromagnetic frequency of the planet but they are useful in an emergency.

"Thank God for cell phones," he thought ringing Rowena back.

But after hearing the words "this network is unavailable" the once-sung hero of the mobile phone was now being cursed.

"Damn these stupid phones," he shouted.

"Try again," I said.

Matt tried several more times with no luck.

"Ring your mom."

His mom came to mind. The thought of her made Matt regret how he had treated her over the years, hardly contacting her, never telling her he loved her, feeling inconvenienced rather than pleased when he had to go and see her for whatever reason. He didn't even know if he had her number in his phone. But this was the story of his life. He didn't really have much time for anything or anyone except work.

"Where are you mom? Where are you? Where are you?" he said, as he finished scrolling through his address book for a third time. But he didn't have her number in his phone, and he certainly couldn't remember it because he hadn't rung it enough.

"Jesus Christ," he cried.

Matt was upset and started getting angry.

It had crossed his mind that he may never speak to his mom again if he didn't get out of there and he remembered less than an hour ago the e-mail he received and the opportunity to tell her he loved her in his reply. He thought it odd that he would have even considered writing "I love you" in his response. He turned again to his only friend, **The Earth Guide Book,** which said:

"Make sure everybody you love knows you love them just in case you don't have time to tell them before you or they die."

"Am I gonna die?" he said, reading a line he'd already seen once today. The universe was trying to tell him something. "This is a nightmare."

"Go find another phone Matt," I told him but he didn't hear me.

The floor outside Matt's new lodgings was getting darker and darker, like someone was gently pulling a blind down on the sun as the smoke slowly hunted its prey, down the corridor, outside his door.

9:40AM

He started thinking time was running out fast and if they didn't put out the fire soon he might not make it out. It was mad for him to stay still now, just waiting. He figured there wasn't a rescue party on its way and the time he had left in this room, if he had any chance of survival, was probably minimal. But he couldn't move just yet. He just couldn't physically bring himself to face the smoke and the fire and possibly death. Not yet. Bravery was not his strong point, unfortunately. Joining the F.D.N.Y., like me, would have been Matt's worse nightmare.

The concept of death had been relegated deep to his subconscious mind. My heart attack had been successfully erased. Why would he want that on screen saver when he could hit the delete button and it was gone forever? But it hadn't gone and he was now faced with a "do you really want to empty the contents of your recycling bin?" moment. But he had no choice. The contents were being emptied for him, out of panic, as his mind scrolled through itself looking for bits of information to make him feel better. Something he might find on file, saved on hard disk, under "death" maybe, that might help him in this situation.

Then he found it. The date saved was 8th December 1980. My death day or as we say here rebirth day. He recalls it.

Matt is playing music with his brother and happens to glance out of the window just at the right time. He sees me stop washing the car and clutch my chest. I take my final breath and he hears me gasp. He hears the death rattle that gave him nightmares for years. A few seconds later I am on the floor. Matt screams, "Dad," to Luke and rushes outside followed by Luke.

Matt screams for his mom, my wife Win, who comes running hysterically.

"Dial 911," she cries.

In the hospital a medic in a white coat arrives who says, "I'm sorry but I think your husband must have died before we got to him. There was nothing we could do to revive him. I'm so sorry."

Matt, very solemnly, asks his mom if he can see my body and she says no.

Matt runs out of the room, down the hospital corridors and finds his way to the open air of New York.

He lifts his arms up towards the sky and the feelings now emerge from deep within him and into the cold air he shouts "Noooooooooooo!"

Replaying my death only made him feel better in that he thought if I could go through it so could he. Matt likened my death to a public execution, as the whole family looked on, so surely he could manage it on his own, in the privacy of this room, high in the sky in the south tower, if need be, he thought.

He also thought it was probably harder for those left than the one going. After all when you're dead, you're dead and you don't know anything about it. Matt was in for a big surprise. In his desperation and indecision Matt started praying. Words that had no real meaning to him, that he'd learnt as a child, just tumbled out of his mouth.

This was a great shock to him as it was to me, as he was totally non religious, in fact almost anti. But here he was now, twenty years on since his last prayer, desperate and wondering if it was worth another shot. I reminded him of how he and I used to pray every night to God and say thank you for all the things we had. He had loved praying as a boy, not because he was religious but because he was doing it with me and it made him feel good and safe and loved and warm inside. This was a feeling he desperately needed right now so without thinking he clasped his hands together and started praying.

"Dear God, if you do exist, you gotta help me buddy. I'm stuck in the south tower of the World Trade Center and I need to get out to see my wife and beautiful kids. I'm sorry I haven't prayed to you much for the last twenty years but I will now if you get me outa here. I promise."

This would be a deal with God hundreds of victims of this disaster were making right now, whether they were in one of the financial centers themselves, or at home watching it all unfold before their eyes, knowing a friend or relative was in danger.

"Our Father, who art in heaven. Hallowed be thy Name. Thy kingdom come. Thy will be done, On Earth as it is in heaven. Give us this day our daily bread. And forgive us our trespasses, As we forgive those who trespass against us. And lead us not into temptation, but deliver us from evil. For thine is the kingdom, the power, and the glory, for ever and ever. Amen."

That helped. Matt felt slightly less panicky as his focus was taken away from the situation at hand. He was amazed he could remember the words of the Lord's prayer but the repetition of them as a kid meant they were very difficult to erase from his mind.

Let me tell you a few facts about the mind. The mind is like a computer and can, when pushed, remember events and information that has been stored there for years. Even after you die it can still remember. So it's advisable to cultivate a positive mental attitude and good mind while you're on Earth. That way you'll have a better life and afterlife!

It is important to recognise that the mind creates your world because what we think and believe about the world becomes manifest in it.

It is possible to program the mind and therefore reprogram it which can be very useful especially when negative beliefs have been taken on board. By reprogramming negative beliefs through such techniques as hypnosis or neuro-linguistic programming (NLP) you can change your outer world. In other words changing your thoughts will change your life.

A small wisp of smoke had penetrated Matt's Berlin Wall type construction and when he noticed it filtering under the door a feeling of dread gripped his stomach. What else could he find to stop the smoke? There wasn't anything. He half attempted, with a few bars of chocolate, to fill the gaps but it wouldn't be long before they started melting as it was getting hotter by the minute. Matt could also hear a crackling noise. Matt assumed one thing—that fire was close. What should he do? Hold tight for the firemen to find him for a bit longer? Would they be able to get up there? Brad had said it was impossible to pass. Would they be able to manage it? And if they could manage it would they be able to get him down? Or would the fire get to him first?

"There isn't a God, is there?" he said out loud but in a quieter, more defeated tone, watching the smoke, hearing the screams outside, feeling the fear. "If there was he wouldn't allow this to happen. God cannot exist because if he did this is just cruel. Or are you punishing me God for not praying to you after you took my father away?" he said lifting his sunken head. "Are you a cruel God?"

Matt remembered the final prayer he had made to God. As a devout Catholic, which I'm not any more, as there is no organised religion in the spirit world, I had taken Matt to Lourdes when he was eleven just before I died.

I am holding his hand and we are standing outside St. Bernadette's grotto where Bernadette saw the vision of Mother Mary.

"What shall I do dad?"

"Pray son, pray for something good," I say squeezing his hand. "God is listening."

Matt lets go of my hand and moves forward in the line. He holds out his hand and touches the rock. He closes his eyes, like he's just seen the man before him do and starts praying in silence.

"Dear God, please don't let my mommy or daddy die. I would be very sad if they did because I love them so much. Thank you. Oh and please let me be picked for the school soccer team as well."

He steps forward following the line out towards the holy water bathing area and bravely whispers these words to the statue.

But it wasn't long before God went on and let him down. Shortly after that trip I died and just to sink the final nail in the coffin he didn't make the soccer team either. He decided that God and prayers didn't work, religion was stupid and there was nobody out there answering any prayers whatsoever. As far as young Matt was concerned, God, as he knew him, did not exist.

His thoughts sent him into a desperate frenzy. Matt sat with his back against the wall, his hands clasped tight and his head bent down. He then remembered a recent event and started feeling very guilty about it and wished it had never happened.

Matt and Tracey are in the underground parking lot for the south tower. Tracey walks slightly ahead of Matt, who is finding it hard to walk in a straight line. He is guided by her wiggling butt towards the car. Sex is the only thing on his mind. Soon Tracey and Matt are up against the side of the car kissing. It feels good. Blood is rushing to all the right places. She makes him feel like a man. His hands find her bottom then explores the rest of her body.

"Rowena, I'm sorry baby. Please forgive me. I love you. When I get outa here I'm gonna make it up to you and I'm gonna leave this stupid shitty little job and we'll have some fun and we'll get married again and we'll start over," he said lifting his head towards the window then slumped back down to the floor in exhaustion.

"Forgive me father for I have sinned...Forgive me father for I have sinned..."

There was a very, very long pause. All the times he'd felt bad or guilty, or that he'd done something wrong, came up. His Catholic upbringing and deep seated beliefs ran deeper than he thought and when it came to his own mortality and spirituality unfortunately Catholicism was his only point of reference. But Catholicism or no Catholicism it is human nature to want to be forgiven when you think you've done something immoral.

He didn't quite know where to start. He started crying. It had been a long time since he'd cried. Matt did anger not tears—in his opinion a much more manly way of expressing his emotion, but it wasn't in truth.

"Forgive…me…father…for…I…have…sinned…" He took a deep breath.

He remembered times when he'd shouted and hit the children when he was stressed, when he'd caused arguments, made Rowena cry, lied, his recent affair. A whole list, that was incredibly painful to start remembering, surfaced and the feelings along with it.

"Forgive me father for I have sinned…" His tears continued. "I haven't loved my children enough. I haven't loved my mother enough. I haven't…loved my family enough…I haven't…I haven't…I haven't loved my friends enough…I haven't…I haven't loved….loved…" Matt cries like a baby.

"Yourself enough?" I said finishing his sentence.

"Forgive me father…for I have sinned. I am a sinner and I'm gonna die. I deserve to die. Kill me then God. Kill me. You're right I deserve to die so just kill me." It is a torturous moment for Matt trapped alone with nothing but his own memories, no computer or work to distract him. I am kneeling down beside him feeling his pain. On the one hand I am pleased he is having these self-realisations but on the other it is painful to see him in such emotional agony.

Matt was tempted to just give up, smash the window in his room and throw himself out. He was also realising that his chances of escaping this now raging death trap were slim. The smoke billowed outside and the temperature inside his potential tomb was on its way up to reaching astronomically high levels.

But instead of throwing himself he threw **The Earth Guide Book** at the wall and it fell to the floor open at the page which said:

"You are forgiven. Move on."

The words gave him the comfort he needed and the third force to start moving. Matt put his clothes back on, despite the fact it was really hot. He also thought it would be a good idea for his clothes to be wet in case he came across any flames. The cans of soft drinks he'd used to barricade the door acquired an additional use. One by one he threw the liquid over himself, even over his head to help prevent his hair from singeing.

A fizzing wet, sweaty, mess, Matt knew that if he was going to survive at all he had to rescue himself and find a way down. His family were strongly in his mind and I kept repeating to him, over and over "contact your family, contact your family" because I knew that if Matt managed to do this before he died it would make his transition so much easier and he'd feel so much better about himself.

Slowly dismantling the barricade, my son, covered his face with his wet shirt and prepared himself mentally to open the door to a smoky corridor, not knowing how bad it would be.

9:47AM

Matt moved quickly but the smoke was all-consuming and he knew he couldn't travel very far without taking a break for air somewhere. The sprinkler system in the ceiling, that should have been on by now, I figured, was crippled by the crash cutting off the water supply.

He passed an empty office with glass walls still intact. What drew him into it, however, were the phones on the desk. Not just one but three. Jake and Tom flashed into his mind.

This was the first time he'd really thought about his boys. "I have to ring them," he said to himself.

The room wasn't as smoky as the corridor yet so he tried the door and it opened. It was an accountant's office, which was obvious from the number of files marked tax and IRS stacked neatly in chronological order on the shelves. The desk looked untouched and he figured its owner, luckily, had not yet arrived to work, unless he had tidied up before he left, which being an accountant Matt thought very possible.

He shut the door behind him and lunged for the middle phone. There was no dialling tone. "Damn," he said picking up the next phone. There was still no dialling tone. "Come on," he shouted as he picked up the final phone, relieved to hear a heart-warming purr coming through the receiver.

First he dialled Rowena's cell but there was no answer and for some reason her voice mail didn't kick in. He then dialled the house phone in case she had managed to get home.

Jake's little voice came on the machine as a recorded message. "Hi you've reached Matt, Rowena, Tom and Jake. I'm sorry we're not able to take your call right now...oh yeah and please leave a message and we'll call you right back," he said in a very giggly, cute way. This was a message nobody wanted to rub off and something Jake was very proud of. "Beeeeeeeeep..." His son's voice reminded Matt of the morning and how Jake had cried when he shouted at him.

"Hi, it's me," Matt said.

As he was leaving a message suddenly everything around him started sliding. The floor was moving and he could hear a screeching metal-on-metal sound like something was about to give way. Then it stopped. The phone line went crackly.

"I couldn't get through on your cell, honey. Listen, I'm stuck on the erm, dunno which floor. It's chaos in here. I've headed up to the roof to try and get air-lifted, but no joy. I'm trying to head down now. I'm sure I'll be fine. I know I shouldn't say this but just in case..."

The phone cut out. Matt rang back.

"...Hi it's me again. You can't get rid of me that easy. Just in case, I just wanted to say..." The phone went dead again. "I love you." The lines were down.

"Text them," I said. "Text them."

"I LOVE YOU ALL XXXXXX," he typed into his phone to send a group text to Rowena and his children. He pressed send and waited. It didn't go. "Please go, please go, please go," he said very precariously standing on a revolving office chair, waving his arm in the air, like he was stranded on a desert island trying to get help.

He held his phone as high as he could and willed it out of the tower into the ether. Finally it went. In this moment he was glad he had persuaded

Rowena to give in to buying them all a phone for Christmas last year.

As he stepped down from this elevated position he noticed more smoke was infiltrating this glass room and soon he'd be in his very own private gas chamber.

"Your brother, your brother," I impressed upon him.

Panicking he found his brother's number. He hadn't spoken to Luke since New Year and he normally wasn't the first to give, but what the hell. You only live once, or so he thought. Maybe he could do some good there.

9:50AM

Transporting my psychic vision into Lennox Hill hospital maternity department, I could see it was as busy as ever as many new souls made their way into the world, claiming their bodies with which to experience the physical dimension.

Just as the rescue angels help spirits cross back over into the spiritual world, the birthing angels also help new souls enter the Earth plane and I could see at least three of these beautiful beings with Lorraine, as she entered the final stages of labour.

In what looked like a large hot tub two midwives peered in like little children looking for fish. Lorraine was screaming with pain as the contractions, now only seconds apart, rushed through her uterus. On occasion she managed to breathe through one without screaming but inside it took all her inner strength and mind to control it.

Luke was beside her, in his swimming shorts, holding her hand.

"Owwwwwwwwwwwh," she screamed.

"Just keep breathing and try and relax into the pain," one of the midwives said.

"Like they taught us at the classes darling," Luke said seeing Lorraine in agony, feeling secretly pleased he wasn't a woman.

"You try...owwwwwwwh!"

Sweat was dripping off her and she'd reached stage two of her labour already. Her cervix was fully dilated and her contractions thirty seconds apart.

The new soul, Abigail, who was about to take her first breath on the planet remained quite calm, considering the circumstances. She is a girl this time round and I got the feeling she'd come quite quickly from another lifetime as a male Korean soldier. Her new human mind would have no conscious memory of that lifetime however, as she was here to have a very different experience of the world.

Abigail was manifesting as a very small point of light and hovering, with her guide, just outside the tiny body Rowena's body had miraculously created for her. This was going to be her home for the next 87 Earthly years changing and developing as she too changed and developed.

No-one Earthly could see this nor could they see the three angelic presences in the room, helping create the tunnel from the spirit world to the Earth.

"You're doing great Lorry," Luke encouraged.

"This is killing me!" she screamed, wanting it to be all over.

"You're almost there," Luke reassured.

"I don't think I can take much more."

"Keep going baby. You're almost through."

A strange face popped her head around the door and summoned one of the midwives out. She looked quite alarmed. Luke could only assume there was another birthing process needing more assistance than theirs, perhaps a real emergency and took it as a good sign that Lorraine was doing so well.

Behind closed doors, however, I could see in the staffroom the TV was reporting the disaster of the World Trade Center. Live on camera Lower Manhattan was blazing.

"Goddamit, hell fire," the midwife said. "My next door neighbour works in that building."

The commentary on the TV kept rolling over, repeating and speculating about the event. A news reporter stood on the edge of world shattering news, probably at the highlight of his career, microphone held tight, with the devastation of the twin towers in the background.

"At approximately a quarter to nine this morning an American Airlines passenger flight crashed into the north tower of the World Trade Center. As if this wasn't enough a second passenger aircraft, approximately twenty minutes later, also crashed into the other twin tower. As yet it is unclear as to why this happened and it is still not known how many people have been killed."

Television sets across America would undoubtedly be being switched on as friends and family rang each other with the devastating news.

Back in the birthing room Luke was interrupted by the tune of his cell which he'd forgotten to turn off after phoning Win. He saw the call was from Matt, who'd eventually been connected. Luke thought he'd better answer it as they hadn't spoken for such a long time. He was going to tell him he'd ring back later.

"Hey man," Matt said composing himself. "It's Matt."

"Hey Matt." Matt heard screams in the background. "What's happening brother?" he asked.

"Lorraine is about to give birth. Can I call you back?" his brother replied.

"Not really. I just wanted you to know that erm, erm I'm sorry about that New Year thing. I was an idiot and…erm…erm…you've been a good brother and I…erm…love you bro," he said.

"Cheers Matt. I love you too bro. You okay?" He couldn't believe it was Matt saying these words.

Lorraine screamed again interrupting any further bonding they may have.

"Gotta go little bro, we'll talk later," he said, shocked but pleased with Matt's apology.

114

Luke put the phone down to concentrate on the new co-creation of joy coming into his life. Tears filled his eyes and spilled down his face as in one last final agonising push from Lorraine, the baby's head popped out and his first child was born. A warm glow filled his heart.

Talking to Luke had made him feel better and back in his borrowed office he felt quite proud of himself for apologising, something he wasn't used to. Saying sorry to his brother wasn't as hard as Matt thought it would be. Why had he held on to that for all those months? He asked himself.

It certainly gives a sense of self empowerment when you make amends for your actions. Matt had little time to dwell on his call however as the smoke was becoming thicker and thicker and he was coughing and spluttering this lethally toxic substance out of his lungs. He regretted smoking now more than ever. His lungs were weak. Mentally he was weighing up the possibilities he had. He knew he had to move again. But did he have time to contact his mom?

"Damn," he thought. "I didn't ask Luke for her number."

But when he tried Luke again, he'd switched his cell off. Matt hoped his mom was okay and that she wasn't anywhere in the vicinity of the Trade Center.

9:53AM

It was highly unlikely that Win would be near the financial district as she rarely went further than Broadway. I found her back at her apartment, in Brooklyn. She had long since finished with the quiz programmes but as usual the TV stayed on to give her a bit of company. She didn't like the silence. The horrific scenes from the financial center flashed up in her lounge. Misty gave a little yelp at the screen as she knew something was amiss. Animals are not as stupid as we think, especially not Misty. Her general knowledge, of course, was spectacular.

Win took her place on the sofa, next to Misty, with a piece of toast piled Everest-high with butter. As Misty remained transfixed on the piece of toast, watching it move back and forwards from Win's mouth to plate, mouth to plate, Win switched channels with the remote. Thinking it could be some kind of action movie, she hadn't yet registered what was on screen and how it would impact on her life.

The commentary continued and as she watched, in the distance, the cameras picked up another aircraft approaching. This was a repeat of what had happened earlier. It was the United Airlines flight 175 from Boston.

"Oh look, Misty, they're sending in reinforcements," she said without taking her eyes off the screen. But Misty was still more interested in the toast.

"Good job we're not there," she continued.

The TV reporter's measured delivery gave way to gradually mounting hysteria.

"Oh my God, there is another plane coming into the city and it is headed straight towards the twin towers. It's going to hit it. This can't possibly be happening. It's heading straight towards the south tower. New York is clearly under attack."

When Win heard the words south tower she leapt out of her seat, much as she did when she knew the answer to quiz questions, but with more gusto.

"Oh dear Lord, please let this not be true. Please dear Lord, don't let my Matt be in there."

She grabbed hold of her Jesus statue and knelt on the floor in front of the television as though it was some kind of altar.

She started repeating the rosary.

"Holy Mary mother of God…" Her prayers went on for a long time while she watched the second plane impact on the south tower, saw footage of people fleeing for their lives and flames starting to fall from the sky.

9:54AM

Images of New York, looking like a war zone, flashed into my third eye. Cars and taxis were finding their way out of Manhattan but weren't allowed back in. Police were everywhere, people united, shopkeepers giving food, water and shelter. Times Square commuters and tourists were reading the electronic banner headlines and there was a mass exodus from the island. Then Rowena appeared in my mind looking petrified. I felt like I was there with her. I saw her running across Brooklyn Bridge, without shoes.

"Can I use your cell?" she asked a plump waddling lady who had just ended a call.

"No sorry," the owner said, fleeing. Starting to pick up pace, she turned her back on Rowena and looked like a duck on the run. Ro tried to use her phone again but with no success. In anger she threw it over the side of the bridge into the river.

She was not defeated, however, and carried on asking. This time she tried the more malleable sex. A man in his late fifties with a camcorder had stopped in mid flight to film the whole event. This will make good TV later. Just wait till the wife sees this, he was thinking. When Rowena interrupted him he didn't let the camera down from his face and instead turned it around to look at her desperate expression.

"Excuse me sir but my phone has broken and I need to contact my husband who's trapped inside that building, like right now. Do you have one I can borrow, pleeease?" she begged.

For him the conversation happened through the lens. She was very tightly squashed in the frame, on 'zoom-in' mode.

"Errm...sorry," he feebly apologised. Reluctantly Rowena repeated her plea adding an extra "please, if you have any compassion in your heart sir you'll help me. I'll even pay you."

"Let her use it!" Delilah shouted at him.

"No problem," he suddenly said, to Rowena's surprise, as he held tightly on to his very expensive and very new piece of equipment. He turned it back to the twin towers whilst he directed Rowena to his mobile which was in the side pocket of his backpack.

Rowena soon had this strange man's phone and was working out how to use it when she realised she didn't know Matt's number by heart. It was stored in her own phone. She couldn't believe it. She was desperate, and returned, like a dog looking for its buried bone, to the edge of the bridge and just stared deep into the water, trance like, until she eventually said,

"Why did you throw it away Rowena? You stupid woman. What were you thinking?"

In the confusion, the heat of the moment and blind panic Rowena had made a big mistake. Time was slipping away. The reflection in the East River showed devastated buildings getting worse – more thick, sickly, black smoke suffocated the World Trade Center.

9:55AM

Looking to the top of the towers hundreds of people in the Trade Center had left their bodies and the spirit rescue operation was now in full flow as they approached the gateway. I knew Doris would be extremely pleased at how the rescue was going.

She had told us earlier in the morning that not everybody would go towards the tunnel; some would flee unaware of their "deadness" and head home to be with their families, thinking they had made it out alive. But if Doris had anything to do with it they would be few and far between.

Inside the south tower Matt peered through the glass door. It was very dark and smoky out there. Whilst crouching down near the floor, hanging on to the door handle, he had a rather unusual thought which he acted upon immediately.

I had suggested that he communicate his feelings of love for his wife a different way. So he took **The Earth Guide Book** out of his pocket, retrieved a pen and scribbled a note on the inside cover to Rowena. He also wrote his home address asking that it be returned to Ro if found, then put it back in his pocket.

A deafening bang speeded up his actions, as part of the roof, a few floors below collapsed. His eyes were smelting and stinging from the smoke. The stench in the building smelled horribly toxic and the temperature was now at sauna level. Sweat poured off him. Dehydration would become an issue very soon but the cans of pop from his retreat room were still keeping him going.

Matt gripped the door handle again, took a deep breath, and counted 1, 2, 3. It was like opening the flue to a chimney. The extra smoke seemed happy to see him and to find a new outlet to explore as it rushed into his borrowed office. As a gut reaction, Matt fell, speedily, to his stomach. He put his face as close to the floor as possible, to avoid inhaling the smoke and crawled along, like a soldier advancing under fire, head down, belly flat on the ground. He wondered where he should go first. Surely it was only a matter of minutes before his body would be overwhelmed with smoke and heat.

I'm gonna to have to risk an elevator, he thought. They get down pretty damn fast. But he figured they would have stopped long ago. He had no idea people were still trapped in them, in both the south and the north tower.

His other option was to try and leave the building from another one of the three major stairwells. In order for him to get to the undamaged one at the other side of Trade Center 2 he would have to trek a long way across the building. But he didn't know it wasn't damaged and therefore didn't know if it was worth the effort. He also wondered whether he could find another floor, less smoky than his, where he could buy more time. Time was running out for him. I could feel it. The smoke and heat were taking no prisoners. Matt could barely see a thing. Covering his face more closely with his rolled up shirt he crawled as fast as he could.

How the hell had he got from waking up this morning in a lovely comfortable bed with his gorgeous wife beside him to this? He didn't know. It didn't make any sense and it made him realise that you really never know what is going to happen next.

If he'd have known the day was going to turn out so badly he would have stayed at home and risked losing his job. And he certainly wouldn't have left Rowena in the elevator for the sake of a couple more thousand dollars a year pay rise. He made the decision that if he did somehow miraculously survive this ordeal he would quit. Tomorrow.

Muffled noises of people shouting, possibly even screaming, drew his attention, but he wasn't sure where they were coming from. He thought he saw movement further on down the corridor. Was it someone in the same situation as him, crawling to survive this sudden, undeclared war? But he had no energy to make any kind of signal, verbal or otherwise, as all his attention was on his escape. He focused on this possible companion in distress as a target to reach within the next few minutes. He looked at his watch and the time said 9:56am. I have to get out of this corridor before 9:57am he decided, giving himself a goal.

The combination of smoking, like a stressed out idiot, for years and giving up his gym membership were a potentially lethal drag on his progress, and he vowed that when he got out he'd be straight back to the gym. But right now it felt like a plug was being pulled out. His whole system was collapsing in heat exhaustion and his lungs were battling to give his body the oxygen it needed. His energy field was dimming fast. Matt needed more than gym time now as his body fought really hard to stay alive and under his command. He had no choice but to stop for a rest.

Dizziness, sickness and dehydration from excessive sweating overwhelmed him as he came to a halt like an old truck with a dead battery. Matt passed a few unconscious moments, his mind dreaming all kinds of nonsense that he wasn't even aware of. Then, suddenly, he had a new infusion of energy and stood up to face the smoke and the dying building.

"Good," he thought. "Thank you body. Now let's get outa here."

This time, however, unbeknown to him, when he stood up, he left behind his 32 years and two-month-old shell, that had carried him on this amazing human-spiritual journey. His physical body had taken its last breath and lay inert, lifeless, on the floor, its job on the Earth plane now complete.

9:56AM

Surprised to find himself standing up his immediate thoughts were to run, run, run, like an athlete through the building and down to the ground floor. His body had found a new strength, a second wind, he thought. If he ran as fast as he could he might stand a chance of avoiding asphyxiating himself, as his lungs wouldn't have a chance to get too full of the toxic smoke, he thought. So like a bullet, he sped through the building heading for the exit.

There were pockets of life on some floors. He knew this because he could hear activity, but couldn't see anything through the smoke. As he flew down the stairs, with me right behind him, he suddenly screeched to a halt, like he'd just been ordered to do an emergency stop in his driving test.

"Wao, Brad," he said. Brad's dead body was now quite stiff, having been left for quite a while. Brad was decorated by two women, one arm over each of his shoulders, piled up on the floor. They were the two women Matt himself had refused to help. Good job he did, he thought to himself, otherwise that would have been him, dead. It all felt so surreal, like he was in a horror film.

"I'm so sorry man," he said to Brad's carcass, pushing away the rising urge to weep—he knew there was no time for it now and that he would have to pay his respects later.

If Matt had bothered to look around he would have noticed the two ladies on their way up the circular tunnel at the top of the stairwell, all in astral form, moving towards the light. But he didn't turn his head, just remained focused on the task at hand which was to leave the building as quickly as possible.

The smoke wasn't affecting him now. He thought his body had built up some special immunity to it or something.

Further down the Trade Center he heard cries. The noises took him to where the plane had kamikazed through the side of the south tower. Many souls would have been released from their bodies on immediate collision. A handful were wounded and miraculously some were fine, just shaken up. A number of people had decided to stay with their wounded friends. An act of heroism and compassion I admired, which unbeknown to them, would ultimately raise their vibrations ready for the next world.

There were others giving reassuring words of comfort, telling one another that they would be rescued soon, being amazingly brave in the full-on shock of the disaster.

"It's okay," he heard one light-worker say to a woman crying with pain from her injured leg. "It'll be okay."

"Please don't leave me, don't leave me," she said not realising she had left her body.

"I won't leave you. I'll stay with you," he reassured. "You'll be just fine. You'll see."

She felt comforted by his words and had no idea he was not of this Earth. He beamed a block of blue healing light into her leg to ease the pain. Because she had not realised her body was dead she was still connected to the pain. She could not see the light, but both Matt and I could. Again he thought he was hallucinating from the chemicals in the smoke, which were obviously affecting his brain.

There were hundreds of spirit guides in the lobby, filling it with love. Matt could see them, all different shapes and sizes and nationalities, mainly the ones that were at the meeting earlier that day. I recognised a few of them as they worked hard for their Earth friends. The most prominent images that stuck in Matt's mind, and mine, however, were the angels. Hundreds of angels glowing with light amidst the terror.

Anybody still alive now who did not make an immediate exit from the lobby would make the ultimate one back home very soon, I thought, as I checked the Earth time which was 9:56am. Just three minutes to go.

There was only one way out of the lobby and a brave young man stood silhouetted, repeatedly shouting to his co-prisoners "over here, over here". A handful of people were able to follow his voice to get to safety down the only stairwell that was left intact.

Matt made his way across the jumbled field of love and death towards this man.

A gaping black hole, where the airplane had blasted its way into New York's Trade Center, windowed a smoky sky which was masking a once sunny Tuesday morning.

Pouring through the collapsed roof, Matt also saw a bright torch-like light which he assumed must have been from the fire-fighters. But he was wrong.

He found his way to the stairwell again and started his descent. The closer we got to the ground floor the less populated the building became. The empty offices were like mini ghost towns with half empty cups of coffee on desks, computer screens still on, jackets on backs of chairs, pens and papers and files all over the place. The only life he saw was that of the firemen, running around checking each and every room for scared or lost people. There were some slower, disabled people being escorted down the stairs. Matt checked they had all the help they could.

"Need any help guys?" he asked a couple of fire-fighters. They didn't acknowledge him so assumed he wasn't wanted and zipped passed them.

Exiting the building at Church Street he was greeted by bloodstained pavements and dead bodies. Bodies that had once belonged to people trapped in the tower, who had flung themselves out in desperation, or passers-by who had been unfortunate enough to be hit by falling debris. A gruesome sight. The north tower was still ablaze, as the south tower started swaying in the sky. The towers did sway on quite a regular basis, especially in high winds but this was okay. It was factored into the design. But today, on this beautiful, wind free day, the deviation from the tower's central point was clearly a mark of devastation to the city.

It would only be a few moments before the tower stopped moving and was forced, under the pressure of the upper floors, to fold in on itself as the steel structures succumbed to the soaring heat.

Matt was in shock. As he looked up, into the ash falling sky, he saw what he thought was a giant angel, overshadowing the towers. Beyond that he saw a white vortex spinning faster and faster.

"What the...?"

I was feeling a little impatient, concerned for Matt's safety in crossing over and was taking my opportunity to make myself known to my son. Now was a perfect time as Matt stood, in astral form, by the railings of St Paul's Church. The sun behind him was casting its shadows over the gravestones but he stood shocked and shadowless, his mouth wide open, watching the sky, watching the tower, watching the chaos all around him.

I descended closer to the realms of the Earth plane, feeling the harsh solidity of its vibration, not liking the density, but knowing that I had no choice. I had signed up for this job when I decided to come back and be a guide to Matt. There was no going back. Not that I wanted to, because Matt was more precious to me than anyone right now.

I surrounded myself mentally with golden light as I landed on the astral plane in front of him. The tunnel of light to the next world was behind me waiting to take its next passenger home. Two gatekeepers stood at the edge of the light vortex, like the queen's guards protecting the entrance.

I stood in front of him on the Earth plane. This was as low down in frequency to the planet I had been since the day I left. I ignored the fire department frenzy, the hysterical New Yorkers, and concentrated solely on my son.

"Matt," I said to him. Matt just looked straight through me. I managed to squeeze my vibration a bit further down and become even more solid.

"Matt," I repeated more loudly, more lovingly.

Matt locked on to me and just stared, wondering what reality he was in, what had happened to his brain. Would he ever be the same again? Would he be a casualty of war with little or no brain function, or was post traumatic stress syndrome setting in already? Or was he really seeing his dad? That's what he was wearing when he died, he thought. He remembered my brown trousers. It couldn't be him. His dad was dead. All these things bounced around his head. I held my hand out in front of Matt for him to take.

"Dad?..." he questioned, not moving from his safe spot. Just looking.

"Matt you have left your bo...". I was interrupted by shouts from behind as a man fleeing from the blazing building, covered in wounds and burns, staggered onto the street shouting "run, run, run." His physical body rushed straight through Matt's energetic one.

Matt felt a shudder, but nothing more, and his focus was now distracted, from what he thought, was an illusion of me, as the south tower started to move, slowly at first and then suddenly the almighty, concrete avalanche began.

"Ruuuuuuuuuuuuuun," Matt screamed, along with half a dozen others, as he took off down the street, now free of the constraints of his body. No more beer belly. No more wheezy breathe from his lifelong nicotine addiction. But he'd forgotten about all that. He was just caught up in the moment as his astral legs moved him rapidly down Church Street away from the terrorist's successful demolition of World Trade Center 2.

Offices became bricks, became rubble, became dust. Filing cabinets, fax machines, computers, light fittings, elevators, vending machines, telescopes from the observatory and, worst of all people, all came toppling down. Destroyed within ten seconds.

9:59AM

The south tower collapses

9:59AM

The steel structure of the building had finally given in to the torturous pressure of the white hot temperatures. The attackers, whoever they were, had planned their job well. The fuel from the planes was burning, and no doubt, somehow, extra fuel had been smuggled on board, to make sure the touch paper of the tower was lit, a hundred times over, leaving no room for a failed mission.

Despite the absolute terror that had emerged from the financial area, I could still feel the healing energy moving swiftly across, from the other side, to help those still holding on to life by their finger tips, to let go. Angels were also there for those running, who were fated to run the wrong way. Matt was sprinting at high speed because he was so light now without his body. He thought it was an adrenalin rush, and he'd heard the tales of men picking up cars, out of sheer determination, to rescue their loved ones. In this moment he felt he could do the same.

Faster, faster, faster he ran. The bricks swept up like a wave behind him. He was still running but he was running on top of the debris, at the edge, surfing the building—an absolute impossibility to someone who was alive. His astral heart was pumping his astral blood around his astral body.

Matt couldn't believe how fast he was heading out of the financial district, and thought if the tower had been falling, rather than collapsing, he wouldn't have stood a chance of escaping. Still not giving in to the fact that he was dead, he ran ahead of the other escapees fleeing for their lives towards Midtown.

Matt screamed "run" again at the top of his voice. Nobody in the Earth dimension heard him but everyone in the other dimension did. The spirit rescue workers, aware of the tower's fate and waiting for its collapse watched, as this iconic New York giant was slugged to its knees. They then moved in to help people cross over to where they would be greeted by deceased loved ones in the spirit world.

9:59AM

I wondered where Rowena and Delilah were, knowing that if they could see this it would be dreadful. So by tuning in to their vibrations I found them still on Brooklyn Bridge with a crowd of other frightened New Yorkers and tourists.

Rowena looked on across the river, unable to see much but a thick cloud of greyish white dust. She knew that it was the south tower falling. She watched in horror, transfixed in the road like a statue, as though looking back had cast a spell over her. In those forever seconds, minutes, hours—however long it was she didn't know—the feeling inside her was just numbness. A contradiction maybe, but there was no feeling, just an image of destruction before her eyes. But when the thawing eventually came so too did the questions. Was Matt in there? Was he dead?

Delilah knew there was much more to it than that. Like the rest of the world Rowena was in shock. As guides cannot be seen, except by a few gifted individuals, Delilah could do nothing more than hold Ro's hand and send her positive, loving healing energy.

Rowena's feelings now surfaced and sank their claws into every single cell of her body. Nausea rushed through her stomach. She could not stop herself from being sick. With one hand up against the bridge supporting herself, the other holding her stomach she puked and puked, holding the thought that Matt was probably in the building. Holding the thought that she might have been in that building, that others, with wives, husbands, children, friends would be in that building.

The man with the camcorder had disappeared leaving her with his phone, but she didn't care. She couldn't care less. The sickness kept coming in waves. This was an unfamiliar feeling. Normally strong in a crisis she was being defeated. She felt like her knees too had been kicked from behind and she was now crumbling.

I wondered whether those responsible for this monstrosity had created a lot of bad karma for themselves.

The Earth Guide Book says about karma:

> **"Karma is only accumulated when in physical form.**
> **The law of karma basically means you reap what you**
> **sow, or whatever you put out there you will get back.**
> **Karma can be worked out through service or through living**
> **karma and will always be balanced out somehow in the end."**

10:07AM

From Rowena I tuned in to Doris to see if there were any further instructions. She was interacting with all her workers. Guides were working frantically to do the right thing. This was a big test for everyone. Many hundreds of spirit rescue workers held their hands out towards their brothers and sisters. A haze of white light hovered over the fallen building as the light-workers merged together, with a radiance so bright it could have lit the way to Bethlehem for an age.

Crossing over was disorientating, but also a relief to many who didn't believe in a life after death. This was a new beginning.

Doris was well aware of the important task of rescuing those inside. She sent more angels down to ground level to help those in need. The rubble piled high. The smoke, like thick fog, devoured the streets of Manhattan.

As predicted by the rescue workers, many souls who'd left their bodies chose not to cross over but instead headed straight home to their families. Some knew they were dead, some didn't.

"We have to follow every single spirit," Doris commanded.

The Great Angel already had her team lined up for that. They were the most highly trained Special Forces workers of the spirit world, who could handle any kind of energy anywhere, whether it was like trudging through thick oil or gliding through air.

"Find them and bring them home. Do whatever is necessary," she instructed.

Approximately 2,800 were due back today.

At least another three hundred rescue workers swooped down to the Earth plane and chased their assignments, as they fled, into the city. I was on the same mission, following Matt as he ran.

10:09AM

Back at Win's apartment Misty looked wide eyed at Win. She had known something was wrong even before Win. But Win's stomach was churning over and over to the pace of the prayer mantra she was reciting to Jesus.

"I believe in God, the Father Almighty, Creator of Heaven and Earth. I believe in Jesus Christ, His only Son, our Lord. He was conceived by the power of the Holy Spirit and was born of the Virgin Mary. He suffered under Pontius Pilate, was crucified, died, and was buried. He descended to the dead. On the third day He rose again. He ascended into Heaven, and is seated at the right hand of the Father. He will come again to judge the living and the dead. I believe in the Holy Spirit, the Holy Catholic Church, the Communion of Saints, the forgiveness of sins, the resurrection of the body, and life everlasting. Amen."

She continued.

"O my Jesus, forgive us our sins, save us from the fires of hell, and lead all souls to Heaven, especially those in most need of Your Mercy. Amen."

The TV still churned out reports of the battlefield scene in Manhattan, giving a minute by minute account. The image of the south tower collapsing filled the screen.

Win picked up the phone and dialled 911. She was always quick to dial 911 at the best of times for any slight disturbance to her self or her neighbourhood, and in all honesty she was a little bit slow off the mark today.

A lady at the other end gruffly answered with the usual spiel before answering Win's bombardment of questions.

"My son works in the south tower. How do I know if he's alright?" she cried.

"We're doing all we can madam to locate missing persons," she replied.

"His name is Matt Moretti," Win pushed.

Win didn't really know what 911 would be able to do, if anything, but she felt she had to do something to try and help. But she hung up before the lady could say anything back to her, and started pacing up and down her front room with nervous energy. Misty followed hoping she might be going for a walk.

With all the events blaring away in the background she scrambled around in a drawer eventually finding an old scruffy address book that she'd had for at least thirty years.

"Matt, Matt, Matt," she mumbled as she thumbed her way through the alphabet. Landing on Matt's name she keyed his mobile number in to the phone. The answering machine clicked in:

"Hi this is Matt. I'm sorry I can't talk to you in person. Please leave me a message and I'll call you back when I can...*beep.*"

It was so lovely to hear her son's voice. It made her feel that he was still alive. She hated answerphones. She'd only just managed to work out how to record things from the TV. Technology and Win were two words that should not be together in the same sentence.

"Hi Matt it's your mom. Please ring me and tell me you're okay, honey. I've seen the news and your building. I just pray that you weren't in there, honey. Ring me. I love you, mom." She put the phone down, after signing off her name, like she was writing a letter, then collapsed on the sofa with frustration.

A few seconds later her phone rang. As she dived onto it, Misty barked, as usual, at the noise.

"Hello. Matt?" Win hoped.

"No mom, it's Luke," my other son said joyfully.

"Luke," she acknowledged.

"I'm ringing to congratulate you. You're now the proud grandmother of a seven pound six ounce baby girl," Luke boasted.

Win was silent for a few seconds then finally managed to pull it together and sound happy. She was, of course, but the celebrations of new life coming into the world were being overshadowed by feelings of dread of Matt possibly exiting the world.

"Oh congratulations Luke, I'm so thrilled," she said mustering up her enthusiasm for his sake.

"Do you wanna come down and see her?" he encouraged.

"Erm, yeah, you try stoppin' me, but not today, it'll be too crazy down there surely," she said.

"Why?"

Luke obviously hadn't heard. He'd been cocooned in his little birthing pool for the last five hours, free from the world and its traumas.

"Haven't you heard?" Win asked.

"Heard what?" he replied.

"Oh Lukey, sweetheart, it's so bad. I'm so sorry to tell you this on such a joyous day as well, please forgive me," she rambled.

"What mom? What's happened?" Luke was perplexed.

"One of the World Trade Center towers has collapsed, and both have been hit by planes," she relayed reluctantly, not wanting to spoil his moments but feeling she had no choice as he'd find out sooner or later.

"No shit!" Luke cried.

"Yes, shit," she mirrored.

"What about Matt. Is he …" He stopped in mid flow remembering the call he'd had from him. "I got a call from him not that long ago."

"What did he say?" Win was excited.

"It was kinda strange. He apologised for the New Year thing and told me he loved me."

Win's heart sank. This was so out of character for Matt, she knew he must have been in danger but neither of them really wanted to go there. After a long pause Win said, "I'm sure he's alright. He'll call when he gets home."

"Yeah, he probably will." Luke didn't sound convinced.

"Anyway, you have a little daughter to think about now," Win reminded him. "Just concentrate on that."

"Yeah I do. I'd better get back. Lorraine is exhausted. Speak to you soon mom," he replied, now feeling a mixture of elation and grief. "Let me know if you hear anything."

Win sat back down on the sofa, put her head in her hands and sobbed. On some level she knew Matt was no longer on this Earth plane.

10:11AM

Ifollowed Matt through the city. He had kept running and running without stopping for breath. He didn't need breath anymore but still he didn't notice. Matt kept seeing strange things on the astral plane and wondered what was going on in his head. Spheres of golden light were shooting passed him like tennis balls. He watched one of them travel into the distance and disappear around a corner. It knew exactly where it was going. These were rescue spirit guides chasing their disembodied friends through the streets.

Those people who choose not to cross at the exact time of death are trapped in an in-between world called the shadowlands. A spirit sometimes does not cross over straight away. One of the most common reasons for this is that they do not realise they're dead. Especially if their death has been caused by a sudden trauma, like a disaster or a car crash, for example. They continue home, as though nothing has happened and then wonder why their family members can't hear them. Once they do realise it a number of things can prevent them from crossing. One is fear. They see the light, feel the pull of it and then get scared thinking that, if they move towards it, it will swallow them up or send them to hell, if they believe they have not been a good enough person during their lifetime. Others just don't know what the light is and therefore don't go anywhere near it when they see it. But there's absolutely nothing to worry about. When I crossed I felt so serene and peaceful and safe.

Matt hadn't crossed yet. His mind was starting to think of Rowena, where she was and what she was doing. He was sad he hadn't managed to talk to her again on his mobile, and wondered whether she'd got his text message.

Matt was looking out for a pay phone as he knew he had to tell his family he was alright, as soon as possible. He was waiting by a public telephone booth and couldn't help over hearing a large black lady shouting down the receiver.

"Oh, Jackie, you would not believe it. I was gonna go in there for dinner today with Rose and the whole building just collapsed, evaporated into nothing. I am so lucky to be alive but believe me there must be thousands dead, honey. Thousands. I think I must have a guardian angel on my shoulder. Praise the Lord," she blurted.

There was silence for a while as she listened.

"Ah-hah...ah-hah...ah-hah...mmm I knows what youse is sayin' honey...ahah.. No way...two planes, my God...Terrorists...That George Bush...I bet he's behind this...ah-hah."

Matt was getting impatient. She was also smoking, which didn't help. It made him want one. With all the hormones pumping around his body, he hadn't wanted a cigarette, but now he could murder one.

"Excuse me but you gonna be long?" he asked her.

She just ignored him. Not out of rudeness or anything else but because she couldn't see him. As far as she was concerned there was nobody waiting.

She carried on talking, which made Matt angry.

"Hey lady," he shouted, "get off the phone. I have my wife and kids to call." Matt's face was up real close to the booth now but again she had no idea he was there and just carried on.

Matt couldn't believe how rude she was and said it one more time.

"Hey lady, you've been on there long enough now. There are other people wanting to use the phone." Again, no response. Matt was fuming.

He tapped her on the shoulder. She didn't feel anything so he straightened his hand to slap her on the back, drew his arm back…then…slap. His hand made contact with her physical body but went straight through it. All the way through her rolls of *Coca-Cola* and waffles-fed fat to the wall of the phone booth. Matt fell forward with the swipe.

"What the…?"

She shuddered like someone had walked across her grave.

"Oooh I'm going all tingly. I think I'm a bit shaken up," she said.

Matt repeated his process, again his hand went all the way through.

"Oooh it's happening again. I think I'd better go. I'll see you soon sweetie," she finished off.

She hung up the phone, threw her half finished cigarette to the floor and left. Matt looked at the cigarette and at the phone. He wasn't sure which one to go for first. Either way he wouldn't win. Now that he was not physical, life had suddenly become very difficult.

Unusually he put his family's needs before his cravings for a cigarette, by reaching for the phone. His mobile must have been lost in the tower somewhere, he thought.

His hand sunk into the atoms that made up the receiver as he attempted to lift it to his ear.

"What?…" he tried again. "What the hell is going on?" He tried again with more force. And again and again and again until he was exhausted. Coming out of the phone booth he screamed, "Noooooooooooooooooooo ooooooooo." It was a good time for me to reappear to him but Matt had other ideas and jumped into a cab, as a guy got out of it, just by him. He was followed by a lady wearing a red feather boa round her neck and a long flowing dress, who'd just stepped off Broadway.

Before Matt could speak she'd ordered the taxi driver to her destination, just down the road from his house, so he didn't argue.

"I can't get back downtown lady, I'm sorry, the police have blocked it and you'd be a fool to go there anyway," he said.

142

"I'll take you to the closest point but this is my last run," he added. "It's gridlocked everywhere so it'll cost you a fortune if we get stuck."

"Just drive. Don't talk," she ordered him. His greasy hair was slapped back across his face. He too had a cigarette hanging on the edge of his lips, almost impossibly like some kind of party trick. Matt wanted it so badly. He listened to the driver coughing that hoarse smoker's cough, that he was developing, and looked at his beer belly, extending so far out it almost touched the dash board.

"I could end up like that," Matt thought to himself but the smoke that travelled into the back of the yellow cab just overrode all that and created even more of a temptation to him. There is something very sinister, very seductive and very evil about nicotine that can capture someone physically and, it now appeared, also astrally. The cravings were still there, because the memory of the physical body was still there, as he hadn't crossed over yet.

The cabbie had the radio on full blast, giving traffic reports on downtown New York, and accounts and speculations of what had happened to the twin towers. Nobody said anything. Matt found himself being drawn closer to the driver and somehow, miraculously, after having the thought about wishing he was in the front seat, found himself in that exact spot trying to breathe in the smoke.

Then the most peculiar thing happened. Matt's desires took him closer and closer and closer to the cabbie and their energies eventually merged. Matt was sitting in the cab driver's body feeling everything he could, including the inhalation of the cigarette fix. "Weird," Matt thought "so weird". Then he started to feel other things like the heaviness in his chest, the pain in his back, slight sciatica down his leg, anxiety about the day, and picked up on the fact that he was worried about his wife, who was in hospital with high blood pressure. But the overall feeling was that of grossness.

"Aaaaaaaaaah, aaaaaaaaaaah, what's happening to me? Somebody please help me? Please," Matt cried as he used all his might to free himself from the confines of his borrowed body. These words fell out of the driver's mouth as he tried to hold them back without success. The expression on his face was one of horror. Seconds later Matt had thrown himself out of the cab and landed in the street.

"Matt," I said gently and firmly, without manifesting myself, as he lay on the sidewalk. "You're dead!"

10:25AM

Matt heard the words loud and clear, like a loudspeaker, in his ears. So I repeated them.

"Matt you're dead!"

As I said them I started to materialise myself into astral form lowering my vibration. And once more I stood before him. Matt stared at me. It was almost like the stare was frozen in place for more than a moment. In his head he questioned if it was really me.

"Dad?" he thought. "It can't be."

"Yes, it's me Matt."

"But you're…"

"Dead?" I said.

"Yes," he said.

"I'm sorry son, but so are you." It was game over for Matt. The end. Or so he thought. It was really only the end of level one.

> **"The Earth plane is the preparation stage**
> **for the rest of one's spiritual journey.**
> **What you do here decides what you will do later."**
> **(The Earth Guide Book)**

"Matt, it's time to go now," I said.

I projected my thoughts upwards and asked for the light to come down so we could return to the spirit plane. Within seconds a brilliant, white, light manifested before us. The intensity of it was huge. Matt just looked at it in awe. Then looked at me as if to say "is this real?" I nodded, then took his hand in mine, like I used to when he was a boy, and together we walked towards the light. As we got closer the magnetic pull became so strong we no longer had to walk, it just lovingly pulled us across and the transition was made.

10:26AM

As we crossed over, Lower Manhattan was being devoured by an industrial smog of ash and smoke. Those in the vicinity of the disaster were covering their mouths and eyes to block the toxins. The general feeling was that if one tower could fall, so could the other. The north tower was due any minute and the second wave of angels and guides hovered close by waiting for the fall.

Then a rumble, similar to the first, began. Everyone knew what it meant and those still in the area started scurrying as fast they possibly could out of the way.

Those that were unfortunate—or fortunate from our perspective—to lose their earthly lives were swept up by assistants directing and shouting them towards the light.

10:28AM

The north tower collapses.

TIMELESSNESS

"How long do you think he'll be asleep for?" I asked Tika, one of theguardians of the hospital, whose job it is to comfort and reassure those who pass over. Sleeping is normal once a spirit arrives here. On waking they find themselves not in their own comfortable bed at home but here in the spirit world hospital.

"I don't know, every soul is different," she replied. "It depends what they have done on the Earth plane and what bonds them there."

She meant that if people had been bad or evil during their Earthly life, then it is likely they may be imprisoned in their own cage of remorse, for quite a while, until they feel ready to look at the mistakes they'd made and make amends.

"I can't imagine your son will be asleep for long. His vibration feels okay to me," she added.

She was right. It wasn't long before Matt woke. He looked around to the lightness of the room which was full of beautiful, vibrant colors. His gaze landed directly on me.

"Dad?…Where am I?"

"Forgive the cliché but you've died and gone to heaven son."

"Am I dreamin'?"

"No son. This is very real."

"Am I dead?"

"Well, your body is but your spirit is very much alive."

"Wow," he replied, kinda shocked.

"How you feeling?"

"I dunno." Matt looked peaceful but confused.

"Is this where everybody comes when they die?"

"Yeah, they come here. It's a hospital."

"Gee it must be well funded."

I laughed. The thought of funding anything in the spirit world was totally impossible. Everything is free. There are no possessions, no money, no need to work to survive. It's such a liberation.

"What else you got here?" Matt asked wanting to know exactly where he was.

"There are many different spheres in the spirit world, son, and you'll eventually go to the one that matches your particular vibration. One sphere is no better than another, just different. You'll find areas of healing, music, arts, performance…There are lakes and mountains and scenery that is so breathtakingly beautiful and alive with colors you've never been able to see with Earthly eyes. It's beyond words Matt. You'll see."

"Who are you?" he asked looking at Tika's vibrant auric field, shimmering with color.

"My name is Tika. I work here in the hospital. I am looking after you," she smiled.

"Oh thanks…" he replied not quite knowing what to say.

"We've been preparing for quite a while for the souls from this New York disaster," Tika told him.

"What about Ro? The boys? They'll be desperate. They need to know

I'm okay." Matt suddenly remembered the horrific day.

"Matt to them you're not okay. To them you'll be dead," I reminded him.

"Jesus Christ! I really have died, haven't I?" he said wanting me to say no it's just a bad dream.

"You've finished your life on Earth, Matt, yes," I replied, softly, not wanting to say "dead" because he was now more alive than he'd ever been.

"But I'll be able to see them again won't I?" His voice sounded really concerned.

"Yeah but don't get too excited as they won't be able to see you. They're not that psychic," I replied. "When you're on this side of life you realise that the veil between the two worlds gives the illusion of death to those left on Earth. They may feel your presence though."

"Will I be able to speak to them?"

"There are ways to communicate, it's difficult, but there are ways. We'll see what we can do," I answered.

"First you have to recover yourself and then complete with the life you've just had," Tika said.

"I'm dead. How much more complete am I gonna get than that?" Matt asked feeling frustrated that his life on Earth had been taken away from him so suddenly. It was even harder right now because he hadn't left it in a state of completion.

"You have to have what we call a life review, Matt," she told him.

"Sounds too much like an assessment to me," he replied. "Are the others from the Trade Center nightmare here…in this…hospital?"

"Yes, that's right, many of them are still asleep," she whispered.

"Is my buddy Brad here?" he asked concerned about him after seeing his dead body on the stairwell and wanting to see a familiar face.

"What was his Earthly name?" clarified Tika.

"Johnson. Bradley Johnson."

She looked at a list, which just seemed to materialise out of nowhere and ran her finger down it.

"No. He's not here yet. But don't worry about him. He'll be found. You have a lot to sort through first," she said kindly.

"How am I gonna do that?"

"There are counsellors and guides here who will help you look at your Earth life and then you can move on," she replied.

Matt lay back thinking about his life, wondering how soon he could get through his review and back to Ro and the kids. He didn't want to be in the spirit world, even though he was feeling the most at peace he'd been in a long, long time. He wanted to be with his wife and children.

"You'll see them again buddy but soon you'll never wanna return from the spirit world and you'll wonder how you ever managed on Earth, dragging your, dare I say, unfit, body around, pushing it to the limits with work, feeding it with junk and zapping it ten hours a day with radiation from your computer or cell phone. Then feeling guilty when you got home because you didn't have any energy left for your family." I reminded him of his crazy, normal working city life existence.

"But I wanna see Rowena and my children," Matt thought to himself.

"I know you do and you will," I said reading his thoughts.

"How did you know what I was thinking?" he asked me, quite put out.

"That's how we communicate now, just with thoughts," I explained. "The mind's like an open book here."

"That's scary dad. Thoughts are personal," Matt responded.

"You can start processing your life as soon as you feel rested enough," Tika said.

"I'm feelin' just fine, thanks. I just wanna get on with it so I can get back," he replied.

"Okay. Galio is ready when you are."

"Who?" Matt questioned.

"Galio. Have you forgotten him? He is one of your best friends. He volunteered to act as a protector for you on Earth. He will also help you review your life when you are ready," Tika educated.

"Great. Where does he hang out then?" Matt asked.

Tika gave instructions as to where to go and without hesitation Matt jumped up to find him.

"You coming to this life review thing?" he asked me.

"I wasn't going to but will if you want me to," I replied.

"Yeah, I would. I'm not gonna see my father drop dead twenty years ago, lose him, find him, then lose him again," Matt smiled.

There was a golden glow coming from under the closed door, which momentarily reminded him of his prison in the Trade Center, but this door was marked "REVIEWERS". On approach it opened automatically, as a voice in his head said, "Welcome Matt".

"Cool," he thought, "automatic doors". He didn't realise he opened the door with his thought about opening it, not because there were any kind of sensors attached.

A very tall light-being stood in a glowing room. In front of us was a reclining chair and on the ceiling was a screen. He acknowledged my presence then turned to Matt.

"Hello, Matt," Galio beamed, overwhelmed with joy on seeing his returning friend. "It's so lovely to have you back."

Matt looked into the eyes of this being who he assumed must have been Galio and almost fell into them. He felt like Galio could read every part of his soul, parts untouched even by himself. After a few stunned moments Galio embraced Matt with the biggest hug ever, and Matt suddenly remembered him.

"Oh my...Galio...I can't believe I'd forgotten you." Matt was overwhelmed with emotion.

"It's hard to remember on Earth. Coming home is like waking up from a dream," he replied.

"Some dream," Matt half laughed in disbelief.

"You will meet many others whom you've forgotten too," Galio said. "They are eager to see you again, but there is plenty of time for that. First we have to look at this dream of yours. Are you ready?" Galio pointed at the chair.

"As I'll ever be," replied Matt as he climbed into it.

SPIRIT WORLD REVIEW

As Matt took to the reclining chair the light in the room dimmed and the screen on the ceiling went from white to black. There were a few mumbling voices of different pitches echoing around the walls in surround sound stereo effect from the monitor. Matt's feelings were affected by the projected images from the screen, and he started to feel warm and safe which he enjoyed for some time. This was a television with a difference, where not just images could be seen, but feelings could be felt too. Feel TV, now that would be an amazing invention for the Earth plane. Then suddenly...Wham! A strong wave of energy interrupted his peaceful state.

"Do you know what's happening?" Galio asked.

"No. It's too dark to see anything, but I feel weird," Matt replied.

"Let me help you." Galio turned the brightness up on the screen.

Now Matt could clearly see himself as an unborn baby still in the womb. The contractions through his mother's uterus were getting stronger and more frequent. This was the energy he could feel which was pushing his tiny body towards his exit. Matt could hear his mom labouring, but her sounds were muffled. He then overheard his final conversation with Galio before he was born.

"You're about to go in again. How are you feeling?" Galio says to Matt's soul.

"I think I've changed my mind," Matt's spirit says half joking.

"Don't worry I'll be with you," Galio reassures him. "But you're not going to remember any of this, like where you came from, how you got here, this final conversation. It's all part of the game remember."

"Well, no, I won't remember will I?"

"No. Probably not until you die," Galio says. "You're going to have a new set of beliefs and a new identity too but the essence of you, your soul, will remain the same."

"Yeah, sure. It'll be strange not being female though."

"Yes but who you really are will never change. You will always be love."

One more push and this new, tiny, male, body that is to be called Matt passes through the dark, vaginal tunnel until it reaches the light at the other end. Nurses and midwives look on as Matt is scooped up and wrapped in a towel. After he takes his first breath the umbilical cord is cut.

**"The birthing process is similar to the dying process but from a higher vibration to a lower one."
(The Earth Guide Book)**

In the review room Matt turned to Galio and said, "you know after seeing that I think I have a vague memory of it."

"Sounds like you are starting to remember," he replied.

"This is so awesome," Matt said feeling totally exhilarated.

"But do you remember why you went to Earth in the first place?" Galio asked.

"No," Matt replied, honestly.

"For experiences," Galio said. "To add to your soul's growth and development."

"I certainly had an experience but I don't think I did a very good job," he confessed remembering his final realisations back in the south tower.

"Who's judging?"

"I am…and probably God…if there is a God," Matt said. "I thought God was punishing me by killing me off in that tower. I thought he'd had it in for me from the beginning, when he took dad away," he continued, looking at me.

I smiled at him and Galio did too.

"You knew your dad might die when you signed up for this life. It was one of your potential experiences," he explained.

Matt didn't know what to say for a while until eventually he said, "Why on Earth would I want to experience that?"

"I've told you to add to the experiences of your soul."

"It's not a game. There are real lives at stake here." Matt was not quite getting it.

"Actually Matt, yes it is. It is the ultimate game," replied Galio.

"And did I sign up for being suffocated to death at the Trade Center in New York too?"

"There was a departure option scheduled for September 11th 2001 Earth time that your higher self decided to take nearer the time," Galio explained.

"What were my other options then?"

"There were two others. You had another ten years or you could go on until you were eighty-six," Galio said. "But you decided to take the early route."

"Why?" he interrogated.

"You had lost the spirit of yourself. Your lower self had taken over and you thought there was no way of returning back to a greater awareness in this lifetime, so you decided to come home earlier rather than later, and the universe allowed it," Galio clarified.

"That's a bit selfish of me. What about my wife and kids?" Matt asked.

"Although they will suffer, it will add to who they are," Galio said. "It is part of their life experience."

157

"I had lost myself. You're not wrong. I was so freakin' miserable," Matt admitted. "What's my punishment then? A spirit world jail where you have to watch constant re-runs of your life? "

"No Matt. There is no punishment. There is only cause and effect which will ripple through the universe and throughout other people's existence forever. Once an act is committed it is there as an imprint on eternity. It cannot be erased. Your actions are very important," Galio said. "And you will feel the effects of them."

"The law of cause and effect ripples through the universe forever." (The Earth Guide Book)

"That makes me feel even worse," Matt replied. "Can't you just send me to purgatory or somewhere awful, for a few months or something?"

"You see this is the effect that the cause has already had on your soul Matt. Why would anything or anyone, even if they had the power to punish you, want to punish you anymore than you are doing to your self already?" Galio questioned.

"I dunno. It's just what we get taught. You do bad, you get punished."

"You see the teachings on Earth are limited because those teaching have forgotten who they are and where they came from, so crazy beliefs are formulated as they try to make sense of the whole scary thing called life."

"So what I did wasn't that bad?" asked Matt, looking for reassurance.

"You're not a major war criminal, Matt. You have to learn to look from a higher spiritual perspective. Let's view your life and see the sequence of events that made your personality, who you were on Earth, and the consequences of the things you did," Galio instructed.

"Okay, if you think that's a good idea, it's cool by me," agreed Matt slightly nervously.

The screen starts moving and many happy baby scenes whiz by. Within minutes we see baby Matt being violently sick and coughing. His body has picked up whooping cough from the local nursery.

"This is the first shock to your system," Galio said.

Also on screen around Matt it is possible to see his aura and the auras of those around him. Matt's aura is dark grey with green speckles. A few weeks later everything is normal again. His field is vibrant and glows again. The seven major chakras, or wheels, of the body, each vibrate with different colors.

There are many scenes of Matt and me praying, going to church, his mom being her usual obsessive, amusing self. Him and Luke playing, scenes at school, doing well, not doing well, falling off bikes. All the usual childhood stuff.

Next on screen we see my death being played.

Matt screams "Noooooooooooooooooooo!" outside the hospital. I am standing beside him and he can see this now.

"Is that you, dad, standing next to me?"

"Yes," I replied. "Before I crossed over."

"I wish I'd known you were there."

"We wish lots of people knew that death is not the end and the spirit of the person lives on. This would not only positively change their behaviour but people would have far less fear of death and therefore life," Galio explained.

"Does God not exist then, because if he does all the suffering people have to go through is not very nice? He ought to go down there and have a go himself," protested Matt.

"It is a complicated subject but a short answer is yes God does exist but not in the way you think. God does not have human characteristics. God does not pass judgements and hand out punishments. No. God is infinite love, light and wisdom that directs everything in the universe and is within everything in the universe. We are a part of God and God is a part of us. God is the force that governs and guides the universe. God is the highest possible consciousness—love." Galio answered.

"So all this religious stuff *is* nonsense. I am right?" Matt gloated.

"If your religion helps you conduct your life in a better way and be kinder to all people then it is good, but there are many failings to religion on the Earth plane, Matt, as you noticed." Galio knew Matt's life inside out.

"I did notice. That's why I didn't get Tom and Jake baptised. I didn't want them to be let down by false promises like I was. I wanted them to make up their own minds when they were older," Matt replied.

"Religion on the Earth plane has regularly been used to make beautiful, loving souls from our world feel guilty, fearful, controlled and shackled rather than empowered. There are so many wars that are fought in the name of God. Wars that torture innocent people, cause limitless grief and suffering. Religion has created disharmony between people, countries, men and women when the truth is we are all one and the same. It doesn't matter what you say you are. It matters how you conduct your every day life. That's what matters," Galio continued.

On screen outside the hospital it is raining and Matt's energy field has completely shrunk and all seven of his major chakras have shut down from the shock and trauma of my death.

Matt starts kicking things. Benches, trash cans, plants, car wheels, anything he can as he walks away from the hospital. He roams the streets for hours, with me by his side. I am feeling equally shocked that I will never be able to speak to my family again and wondering what is going to happen next.

"This event changed your life Matt and after the initial grieving period was over, it was up to you what you did with it. It could have either propelled you forward in life or you could have let it affect you negatively. But the choice was always yours."

**"It is not the event that really affects us but how
we deal with the event, which is always a choice."
(The Earth Guide Book)**

"Well if I'd known it wasn't the final curtain, that pop would turn up one day, on the side of the road after the twin towers had collapsed behind me, in that same uncool brown outfit he used to wear, sorry pop," he grinned, looking my way, "then it might've been easier, but only might've been," Matt complained.

"Yes, it would have been. But you had lost faith. You were hurting. It was hard and your reaction was normal Matt. You wanted to give up on life like many people do and you went home and..."

"Yeah I know. Smashed up my guitar," Matt interjected.

"Yes and this had its consequences." Galio started the film again.

The screen shows Matt coming back into his house. Nobody is bothered about the fact that he left the hospital of his own accord. His family are all in their own places of shock. In his bedroom Matt finds his guitar that he spent the summer months working for. He picks it up and smashes it uncontrollably against the wall. While he does this he cries no tears, just feels an all consuming anger and rage with God.

Matt wept as he watched himself.

"Do you remember the dreams you had as a child?" Galio eventually asked.

"Yeah, sure, I wanted to be a musician like one of The Beatles."

"And what happened?"

"I vowed never to pick up that goddamn guitar again after dad left us." Matt was feeling so sad.

"Your dad, through guidance, tried to encourage you to play again, but you had buried it all so deep that playing became a trigger to a very painful emotion, and you didn't want to go there."

"No, I didn't even wanna think about it again," he agreed.

"This stifled you in two ways, Matt. As music was your main outlet for creativity and made your soul sing, by choosing not to do it anymore it blocked out a large part of your essential self, making you feel depressed. Plus by burying the feeling you had about your dad a part of your energy was always tied up in trying to keep those emotions suppressed. Are you getting the picture?"

"Yeah I was making decisions along the way to suppress myself and as a consequence I couldn't be happy with my life," Matt almost repeated.

"That's right. It's simple. The law of cause and effect at work again."

"So what was I supposed to do buddy? It wasn't my fault," Matt said feeling defensive.

"No-one's judging you Matt. You just made the decisions you made, and as far as it being your fault is concerned, no, the events weren't your fault. But even though it wasn't easy your actions after the events were your responsibility," Galio reminded him again.

"Yeah, I see what you're saying, but it's much harder when you're in it. Especially when you don't know the rules of this crazy goddamn game and everyone pumps you with lies cos they don't know them either," Matt said.

"Figuring out the rules is part of the game too," Galio smiled. "It would have been beneficial for you to continue striving towards your dreams and goals, but Earth is not an easy planet and the human mind is shaped by events and messages along the way. Once your beliefs are formed, the way you live your life is therefore formed too, as your beliefs form your life."

Matt looked at Galio as if to say, "What the hell you talkin' about?"

"In other words what you believe about your self and your world becomes manifest in it. This is another natural law like the law of cause and effect," Galio expanded, still not sure Matt was getting it. "Don't worry you don't have to take all this on board right now. You have an eternity to learn it."

"I just wish I'd known all this when I was alive."

"Do you want to continue or do you want a break, my friend?" Galio didn't want to overwhelm him with too much information. The last twenty-four hours had been pretty mind blowing for Matt.

"No. I'm good. Please continue. I wanna learn and finish as I need to get back to my family a.s.a.p.," Matt said looking over to me.

"There is no rush. Earth is not going anywhere," I reassured him.

"I'm glad about that but I'm happy to carry on, really, if that's okay. I don't feel tired."

This made Galio smile, as no-one ever felt tired in the spirit world, because they did not have bodies to make them tired. Usually during the day Matt would be half asleep at his desk by this point, needing a blood sugar boost from a cigarette or a donut or something else. But here in the spirit world all those physical influences drop away. Once a soul wakes in this world they never have to go back to sleep.

"The universe is an amazing place Matt and you are a part of it and therefore influenced by it," Galio said. "You can even be influenced astrologically whilst on Earth."

"Are you for real? Don't try telling me that a bunch of stars could affect my behaviour? I don't think so," Matt said feeling skeptical.

"I'm sorry but I'm not buying the stars business," he persisted.

"There is much to learn Matt and there is no rush. But you will see. But firstly do you remember what reignited your soul after years of mourning for your father?" Galio asked him.

"Yeah," Matt said, half smiling, thinking of Rowena.

"Love," Galio beamed.

The screen fast-forwards to Matt and Rowena on holiday shortly after they first met.

Rowena looks much younger. They are in a lovely lodge in Vermont. It's winter time and there's a real fire just about burning in the hearth. She is lying on the sofa next to it, reading. A young Matt pushes open the front door with his backside, his arms full of logs, as a cold gust of wind flows through the room.

"Sure you don't want any help?" she offers.

"No babe, I'm fine. You just lie there and relax," he says.

He shuffles across the wooden floor trying hard not to drop any logs. His muscles are rippling, for Rowena's sake. He then throws the wood into their intended pile.

"You're so strong and handsome too," Rowena teases him.

"Well you've either got it or you haven't," he says, as he starts putting the logs on the fire.

Rowena slips down from the sofa and lovingly touches his back.

"Such a strong back," she says. Matt carries on building the fire, lapping up all the attention.

Next thing, they are kissing on the rug. Clothes are starting to come off as their first child, Tom, is about to be conceived.

"I'm so lucky to have a wife like that. She is so beautiful." Matt looked longingly at the screen. "I was so in love then," Matt remembered.

"Yes, you were in a state of love and it helped you come alive again. It was very healing for you."

"Why do we not stay in love?"

"There are many different forms of love, Matt, but the highest form is that which is selfless, where the spirit seeks not for its own gain but to serve wherever it can. You were in a state of romantic love at that stage."

Matt remembered how he just couldn't stop thinking about Rowena and how every minute of every day was consumed with thoughts about her, from wanting to ring her, send her gifts, go round to her work, hold her, kiss her, marry her and have babies and live happily ever after with her.

"I like romantic love," Matt commented.

"Yes, romantic love is wonderful," agreed Galio. "But after that diminishes then you have to keep the love alive by fuelling its fire with selfless acts towards the other, if enduring love with that person is what you really want. What many people do is either move on to the next person, or die a spiritual death within their relationship, by putting up with mediocrity as their love dies and need takes over," Galio explained.

"The problem is humans often confuse love and need," he continued. "And for a relationship to work at its best the love that you have for each other must exceed the needs that you have for one another."

"What do you mean?" Matt was confused.

"We all have needs, right?"

"Yeah," Matt agreed.

"If you meet a woman who you think will meet your needs on every level; who will nurture you, look after you, do anything for you, have a family with you and looks fabulous, then what do you think happens?"

"I fall in love?"

"Yes you fall in love but it's not real love. It's more about projecting your needs on to this woman."

"It is?" Matt seemed surprised.

"And the same for the woman. If she sees you as the muscle-bound, protective male stallion who makes her laugh and can father her children and be a good dad, or he has whatever qualities she desires in a mate, then she will also fall in love."

"So what's the point?" Matt said impatiently.

"The point is once you realise that you cannot meet each others needs then this false love starts to fall away, and you are left with what's underneath. And that could be anything, from a base from which to create true love, to absolutely detesting the person you thought you'd fallen in love with," Galio explained.

"I never detested Rowena, I love her," Matt said feeling defensive.

The screen is set in motion again. A much speeded up version of Rowena and Matt getting married, Jake being born, death scenes of relatives, christenings, Matt starting work, going to the gym, socialising, etc. This initially exciting life soon turns to a fairly mundane one, and the arguments start to become more and more frequent, as Matt becomes more stressed and less happy with himself and the life he has created.

The film slows down to a watchable pace.

It's Christmas Eve. The office party is happening but Rowena is full of a cold and decides not to accompany him. "They're always boring and everyone gets ridiculously drunk," she thinks but doesn't say it. "See you later honey, have a nice time and don't get too drunk," she says instead, as she kisses him on the cheek from her chair.

"You know me," he says.

"Yeah I do. We've got Christmas day to cope with tomorrow," she replies.

At the party, in the south tower there is classical music playing from a four piece string quartet in the corner. Hors d'oeuvres are being passed around by waiters and waitresses on silver platters. It's quite a sophisticated do and Matt is looking pretty sharp in his tux. The best he's looked in a long while, as the tension from his highly stressful job is being melted away by the thoughts of two weeks off over the Christmas period. He already has a glass of champagne in his hand and is chatting with Brad, who is chewing his ear off about work.

"You know I don't wanna talk about work any more," Matt protests.

"Well what do you wanna talk about?"

"I dunno, it's so boring we don't have enough fun in our lives any more. Why don't you tell me a joke?"

"I only know one and it's too rude to tell."

"Go on I probably won't get it anyway."

"Oh you will believe me," Brad replies. "But I'm not lowering the tone."

At this moment Tracey walks over to Brad and says "Hi".

She's looking pretty gorgeous. Tight red dress and a body to die for.

"Oh hi, err, hi, err, how are you?" Brad says stumbling over his words. "This is Matt. He's from the 92nd floor. He was just about to tell a joke."

Matt is put on the spot, but feeling a bit bleary from the alcohol says, "No, I think it was the other way round and I think you just said it was too dirty to tell."

"Oh really," she looks surprised at Brad but then turns to Matt and says, "I'm up for a naughty joke." Matt and Tracey exchange a flirtatious glance. Their auras embrace for a moment.

Matt was somehow able to see all the scenes from everybody's perspectives.

"I don't wanna watch the next bit," Matt said to Galio but he said nothing and let the screen run on.

Matt staggers down the stairwell behind Tracey, occasionally bumping into the wall. He's pretty drunk.

"Sure you don't mind giving me a lift?" he slurs.

"My pleasure Matt," she flirts.

"You know you've got a gorgeous butt," he says flirting back.

"Thank you."

Matt smiles at her back.

Matt and Tracey arrive at the underground parking lot for the south tower. Tracey walks slightly ahead of Matt, who is finding it hard to walk in a straight line. He is guided by her wiggling butt towards the car. Sex is the only thing on his mind.

In fast forward mode Matt saw himself throughout the scene and then the next morning, Christmas Day, trying to be jolly and cheerful, but overly so, as a way of compensating for his guilt.

On screen was another day later in February. It's snowed in New York but has not settled. Everywhere is a bit slushy. Matt is making his way to The Milford Plaza hotel in the middle of Broadway. He seems anxious and in a hurry. Occasionally he looks behind himself just to check who's there. He enters through the revolving doors and goes up the small escalator to the reception area. It's quite busy with tourists and guests rushing in and out, buying tickets for the shows. He sits down on one of the sofas in the foyer and opens The New York Times, while he waits, looking at his watch every now and then.

"She's late," he says to himself.

The room is booked and Rowena knows nothing about it. This is the third time he has done this. The first time he did it he was terrified she would know or that she would find out somehow, but he seemed to get away with it just fine.

So he thought if he could get away with it once he could surely get away with it again, but inside he isn't getting away with anything. The lies and deceit are eating his sensitive soul alive. But he struggles through and as usual pushes his feelings down. He keeps telling himself he is in control.

Then Tracey appears out of nowhere.

"You're supposed to be in the room already," she says over his newspaper, as she sits down next to him.

"You're late," Matt points out.

"I'm worth waiting for," she says sexily.

"You certainly are," he replies folding his newspaper and looking at her lips.

"I thought you should get the key this time. They might start talking or recognising me. We're gonna have to switch hotels soon. Besides that, it's far too busy here," he garbles.

"We decided to come here because it was full of tourists not residents. Stop being so paranoid. Nobody cares," she says rubbing her foot up and down his leg.

"Tracey stop it. You just don't know who's around," Matt panics.

"I'll get the key then and I'll see you up there."

Matt is cringing as he watches this on screen.

"Here is yet again another example of cause and effect Matt," Galio said. "Because your relationship was not doing very well and you had lost the excitement of each other, you took these actions which established its own set of consequences."

Next we are in the hotel room and Tracey and Matt are naked in bed. They've just had sex and both of them are doing the old clichéd thing of having a cigarette, feeling a mixture of sexual relief, relaxation and guilt, although she feels far less guilty than he does. Matt notices bruises on her body but chooses to ignore them.

"We're gonna have to stop doing this," Matt threatens. "Rowena is bound to find out soon and it would kill her."

"She won't," Tracey replies. "Are you sure you shouldn't just leave her? After

all if you're doing this you can't really love her."

"I do love her that's why we have to stop," Matt says, feeling angry.

"You know I have the perfect black mailing tool now," she jokes. "I could get you to give me thousands of dollars to keep quiet."

Matt looks shocked.

"But I won't of course. I'm not that cruel. Anyway I think I'm falling in love with you," she says holding his hand and playing with his wedding ring, gently pulling it backwards and forwards.

"Then we should definitely stop because I'm not falling in love with you. This is just a bit of fun. Excitement. Sex," he says honestly looking her in the eyes which look slightly rejected. "I like you and everything and I think you're fun but at the end of the day, I'm married with kids."

"Don't say we can't see each other again," she begs.

"We shouldn't really," Matt replies.

"But you don't wanna stop do you? You're addicted to me. To the excitement. It gives you something to think about at work, takes you away from your boring, mundane life doesn't it, you sexy hunk?"

She was right but he didn't want to admit it.

"No."

"Let's go do it at The Algonquin next week," she requests. "Like the writers probably used to do."

"I think we should call it a day," he says feebly.

"Oh go on. If you're gonna finish it, we should at least just do it one more time Matt," she suggests. "Don't break my heart. Just one more time."

Matt couldn't say no to her pleas because a big part of him wanted it too.

In fast motion he saw himself going home that evening and getting in to bed and being extra nice to Rowena. She didn't quite understand what had got in to him but didn't mind the extra attention. He saw the mildly amusing journeys to work with Brad and the week passing by at the Trade Center. Finally, he was *at The Algonquin Hotel between Fifth and Sixth Avenue, early one evening. The dark wood panelled décor and low level lighting gave Matt the kind of anonymity he wanted.*

This time Tracey was waiting for him.

"You're late," she jests.

"I've been spending too much time with you," he smiles.

"Have you got the key?"

"Of course and the one to my heart you've got."

"Don't get all heavy on me," he says, secretly loving the fact that such a gorgeous woman might be in love with him.

In the bedroom again, naked, lying on top of her, he says, "So this is the last time then baby. Let's enjoy it."

"Don't ruin it by pointing it out. I'm already upset," she says. As she starts kissing him passionately tears form in her eyes. She is indeed falling in love with him and is very upset he is calling it off, but she knew it had to end one day.

In the review room Matt could feel and sense everything Tracey was feeling, and because he'd had his eyes closed at the time, he didn't know how upset she was.

"She really is upset," he said.

Galio nodded. "She has a human heart."

"I thought she was just in it for a thrill." Matt was very surprised to see Tracey's strong feelings. He was even more surprised to see her sobbing in the hotel room after he had said goodbye and left. She was left all alone when he returned to his family. At the time Matt felt partly relieved and partly sad but mainly thankful he'd never been caught.

Now Matt felt really bad.

"Do you want to feel what Rowena felt when she found out?" Galio asked.

"Not really, no, but I know you're gonna make it happen," Matt replied.

"It would be good for you to know, my friend."

The screen fast-forwards to Matt lying in bed next to Rowena.

"Do you wanna make love tonight, Matt? We haven't done it for ages," she says.

"No, not really. I'm too tired," he replies.

"Are you seeing someone else?" Rowena asks straight to the point.

"No! That's ridiculous. Just because I don't wanna have sex you assume I'm seeing someone else. Well I'm not." He lied three times in the same sentence.

"Why you getting so cross?" she says.

"Because you just accused me of sleeping with someone else. How would you feel?" he replies.

She is silenced by his anger and starts to feel bad for even asking.

As Matt watched the screen he could feel Rowena's emotions.

"I'm gonna sleep in the spare room," he says taking his pillow with him.

Rowena is left in bed on her own, a bit confused by his actions. She's also suspicious and her female intuition drags her out of bed towards his cell phone. There are lots of texts from a T. She reads one. It says: HI! FEELIN GOOD. HOW BOUT U? SAME TIME, SAME PLACE NEXT WEEK? She looks through a few more from this T that are of a similar vein. Then she finds the one she was looking for that says: I'M NOT PREGNANT. THANK GOD!!

"What the hell is this?" she says turning the light on in the spare room and shouting at the duvet.

"What?" Matt says.

"This text. Who is T?"

"Give me that." Matt leaps up and tries to grab it off her.

"You're having an affair aren't you?"

"You shouldn't be looking at my phone," Matt shouts, trying to put her on the

defensive instead.

But she ignores him. "You are, aren't you?"

Matt says nothing. In his head he is trying to weigh up whether it is possible to continue this lie or not. The silence gives him away.

"Matt how could you?"

Rowena leaves the room barely able to contain her feelings. She is shocked to the core. She feels sick and cannot help but shake as she cries.

"You bastard," she screams through the wall. "I thought you loved me."

Matt can feel this now as he watches it all on screen. It doesn't feel good and he wants the feelings to stop.

"Are you trying to torture me by showing me this? I thought you were my buddy," he said to Galio. "I'm sorry for what I did."

"You have to experience how you affected others," replied Galio. "It is important for your learning. If you don't recognise the consequences of your actions you will have a problem in terms of your growth and development."

"Earth is a place of free will which means we can choose what we do, but there are always consequences and in this cause and effect universe no-one ever gets away with anything. I am showing you some of the consequences Matt."

Matt took all this on board. He was slowly starting to realise that his selfish needs and desires had caused hurt and upset to others and this was not the kind of person he wanted to be. It certainly didn't feel good.

"But you also have to remember what I said earlier Matt that people can choose how they react to certain events. It's hard to be so conscious. It takes practice. Not that I'm saying Rowena's reaction wasn't justified. She acted how she acted. And her reaction established its own set of consequences. The same rules apply to Rowena as they do to you."

Matt knew he had carried guilt with him, since the event on screen and he was still carrying it. In his mind he wondered what to do with it.

"Forgive," was the answer that came back into his consciousness.

There were many scenes in his life that touched on that answer but he didn't know how to. Where's the manual that tells you how to forgive? He thought. If only I had that book. In the instant he had the thought **The Earth Guide Book** appeared on his lap.

Galio just kept sending loving kindness to his aching soul. He knew that Matt would figure out how to forgive. He just didn't know how long it would take him and Matt couldn't move on until he did.

Matt opened the book. It said:

> **"Forgiveness does not mean that what you did or what somebody else did was okay, or that the laws of cause and effect can be erased. It simply means that you are willing to let go of the pain you are carrying, learn from it and move on."**

Matt wasn't quite there yet. He continued reading the small print which said:

> **"...we carry around the pain and hurt as some kind of punishment to ourselves or others to make amends. But there is no point in beating yourself up once you have had the realisation that what you did violated yourself or someone else. Learn the lesson and move on, letting go of any negative feelings that you are harbouring towards yourself or others. And then forget."**

Matt read this out loud.

"What is the lesson?" Galio asked.

"Not to disrespect someone else," Matt replied.

"Especially not the person you say you love the most, because this is not love, and it's not very loving toward yourself either, " Galio educated. "Truly loving another is not easy because love has no strings attached, no underlying purpose, is not manipulative and comes not from need. Real love is pure and this is the challenge."

"I wish I could turn back the clocks," Matt sighed.

"By the fact that you are feeling regretful means you are learning. The Earth plane is a place of learning," he encouraged Matt.

"Is that all it is for?" asked Matt.

"There are many functions of Earth and the beauty and magic of being human on Earth is there for everyone to experience. But unfortunately it has become such a lost planet and is a long way from its original state, making living on Earth much more difficult," Galio explained.

"Why?" Matt asked.

"It's down to free will," Galio replied. "People can choose what they do and think and this is not always for the highest good."

"Which then follows the law of cause and effect, right?" Matt added.

"Right. It's better to make a positive contribution to the planet in some way."

"What do you mean a positive contribution?"

"To give to the world somehow so that your being there would make it a better place. Even if it only makes a small difference."

"I don't think I passed that one either did I? I think it'll be a better place with me gone," Matt moaned.

"There are many things you could have done to contribute Matt. There are so many ways to give."

"Shame we don't come with an instruction manual," Matt suggested.

"Yes, that is a good idea. Everyone should be given **The Earth Guide Book** when they are born. Maybe one day they will," Galio said hopefully. "I wonder how many people would actually follow it."

In Matt's life he had battled the selfish, egotistical part of himself against the loving part and unfortunately the selfish part had been winning hands down.

"Please tell me how I make amends Galio and I'll do it," Matt pleaded.

"I am not here to tell you what to do Matt. Once you have the realisations of your actions you will know and will take action immediately."

"Well I wanna go back down to Earth and tell everyone what an asshole I've been and tell them I'm sorry."

"Are you really sorry or would you just be doing it to make yourself feel better and relieve yourself of the guilt?" Galio questioned his intention. "Which defeats the object, and at the end of the day is still being selfish."

"No, I really am sorry man," Matt said knowing Galio knew everything about him.

"Good Matt because your ultimate goal is to become selfless."

The screen fast-forwards with all the after scenes of his affair. Matt telling Rowena the affair is all over, her suspicion, hurt, and scenes of them both acting out their daily lives, but with unspoken issues clouding their happiness.

Then we hear Matt's heart beating so fast, in time to his running feet. Bang, bang, bang, bang, bang, his leather shoes hit the concrete carpet and echo around the subway. Bang, bang, bang, bang, another softer pair of shoes follow him.

"There's only one of them," Matt thinks, as he races towards the exit, stalker in tow.

He heads up the stairs to the dark city night, then down an alleyway, trying to lose him, hoping it would be a short cut to the next street. He soon realises this is a big mistake when he sees nothing but a dead end ahead. The footsteps are closing in on him.

A door to the right looks partially open so without any other option he opens it and goes inside. It is the back entrance to a seedy bar.

Matt is in the basement. He runs through it, still at high speed, passing barrels of beer and cases of alcohol. A man is shooting up crack in his arm. Next to him is a disembodied spirit who was addicted to the stuff when alive, and instead of going to the light decided to stay to carry on his addiction through someone else. Matt couldn't see this at the time, but I could. The spirit doesn't even notice us. Matt prays he is not going to wind up dead in this place.

Loud music is blaring from the top of the stairs and he can see the bouncers outside, pacing back and forth, like they're protecting The White House, or something much more prestigious than it actually is. Another doorway to the left will take him up into the club itself, he assumes.

After some careful, split second thinking, he decides to try and hide himself in the bar as he will be safer in there, especially with people around. If he was back on the street he could easily end up getting a bullet in his back.

Taking a left he runs three at a time up the stairs. Sweat is pouring off him as he bursts through into the bar, realising he had just taken a back entrance on to the stage.

As he charges through the door Matt stands, like a rabbit in headlights, in a spotlight that is meant not for him, but for the half naked woman, dancing round a pole next to him. She barely flinches, like she's used to this kind of behaviour, as he apologises to her.

"Erm, sorry," he says, jumping off the stage.

He pulls his jacket off and then his shirt, under which he has a rather smart but sexy vest, which looks more fitting for this kind of environment. He stuffs his discarded clothes into his briefcase then picks up somebody's half empty drink and pours it over his head to gel his hair back. He turns to the guy next to him, who is wearing spectacles and shouts over the music, "Hey dude, I'll give you three hundred bucks if I can borrow your glasses for the next ten minutes."

"Are you crazy?" this guy yells back.

"Okay, four hundred," Matt screams.

"What you wanna do that for?" he bawls, not trusting him.

"Five hundred that's my final offer buddy," Matt cries, as fast as he can with one eye on the stage door.

"Fine," the man eventually replies.

Matt yanks the glasses off him the second he agrees and puts them on himself. He lights a cigarette, takes a deep breath and pretends to look relaxed whilst *smoking and looking at the woman on stage. Everything is blurred. He cannot see a thing.*

"God man, you're so blind," he says to his new, bought, friend. The guy is now having just as much of a problem seeing as Matt is.

"Give me my five hundred dollars, you weirdo," he says.

Matt's pursuer bursts on to the stage. He has the same embarrassed look as Matt had minutes earlier, but he doesn't apologise, just leaps off stage into the audience. Looking and looking, for Matt. Matt turns his back to him and starts counting out five hundred dollars for his blind friend.

Just as he lays down the final fifty dollar bill he feels a strong pressure of metal in his side. "This is the end of the road for you asshole. Lay off or I'll f****** kill you."

"Who the hell was that?"

"You'll find out later."

Eventually the film reached Tuesday September 11th.

Matt saw the morning's arguments, the train journey to work, spotting Tracey on the way, bumping into Stuart, **The Earth Guide Book***, checking his e-mails. But this time he could see the astral level too, with all the angels and spirit workers occupying the building preparing for the suicide bomber's attack.*

Matt was amazed to see such activity.

"You see Matt, here, in the spirit world, there are many of us who want to serve the Earth plane as it is so precious, and in need of much guidance and healing," Galio informed.

On screen Matt could see me by his side too, which was comforting to him. Seeing himself talking to Rowena on her cell, in the elevator, made him feel uncomfortable, as this was another example of him once more putting his own selfish desires before his wife's needs by not trying to find her.

"I did it again, didn't I?" Matt said.

"Yep," agreed Galio. "If you had gone to find Rowena you might still be on Earth now. You might have taken a different exit time."

"But you said I'd already decided," Matt cross-examined.

"You had but things can change in an instant," Galio said. "Futures can be set but some are also changeable."

"That doesn't make sense," Matt argued.

"You can decide to change your future," Galio explained. "You have to take control of your own life. No-one else will. Your guides don't."

"What do they do then?" Matt asked.

"They just try and help you live the best life possible, according to the goals you wish to achieve whilst on the Earth plane. Some of the goals are set before you arrive on the planet, some aren't," Galio continued.

The screen rolled on. Matt watched himself in the south tower, trapped with his own thoughts and self-realisations, attempting in his final hour to do the right thing before he came face to face with his maker. He saw the smoky corridor and the blocked exits in the building, saw himself crawling along the corridor and then lifting out of his body.

A silver cord connects his radiant astral being with his dying physical one. This cord stretches from his body as he runs through the tower, like a ball of wool unravelling behind him. And just before he turns the corner, to the stairs, the cord comes away from his physical chest.

This was his real moment of death, when his spirit fully left his body.

"People spend so much time worrying about death and it happens real easy doesn't it?" Matt said, surprised.

"Leaving the body is a split second thing. It's not like an agonising battle, its like taking off a glove. It's often when bodies don't die that the spirit has to endure the suffering of being trapped in a painful vehicle," Galio explained.

"It's all so amazing, even death," Matt realised.

"Yes, it is. Life is totally amazing, from beginning to end," Galio smiled.

11:50AM

After Matt's life review I took myself back to Earth to see how Delilah and Rowena were coping. I arrived back at a point where Rowena had, literally, just fallen, into the house and landed on the welcome mat she had bought from k-mart not that many weeks ago.

She was emotionally and physically exhausted. She hadn't heard from Matt since the phone call which got cut off minutes before the south tower collapsed.

Finding Matt was now her overriding priority. She still felt that he was very much alive and hoped he had managed to find an escape route down the tower to freedom before it fell. This may have been wishful thinking on her part but she had to have some hope to keep her going.

The house looked different somehow. The morning's events—screaming, upset kids—lingered in the hallway and at the back of her mind. The fact that this was Matt's home was more prominent. She imagined him coming home from work and remembered how it had been for the last few weeks while he'd been under pressure.

"You're late, honey," she says in sympathy.

"I know. I've had to finish these stats," he says, kissing her mechanically on the head.

"Work seems to be taking over your life right now," Rowena complains.

"I know. I'm sorry. It'll be over after September 11th. We're all preparing for that big day," he says.

Rowena had felt more assured by this response, knowing that there would be an end to the relentless nights of work. She was starting to feel lonely and unloved by him. It felt like he was making no effort to reassure her. But she didn't think it would end like this.

In the kitchen there were still remnants of cornflake droppings on the floor. A bunch of pink roses Matt had bought her one guilty evening, on the way home from yet another late night, had drooped from exhaustion on the breakfast table.

She kicked off her tight, uncomfortable shoes that had played their part in saving her life. She knew she would definitely never wear them again. Unusually, the front door was open, which meant only one thing, that someone else was around. The size five school shoes gave it away. Jake was in his bedroom. Rowena could hear the news roaring from his room. Without hesitation she made her way up to the top floor, climbing each stair as if ascending Everest. This was a conquest in the name of love and support she had to get right for her youngest.

The steps were paved with his clothes, toys and general teenage junk. As she climbed, dishevelled and desperate, she knew that seeing Jake would make her feel better because he was a part of Matt.

Opening the door gently Rowena peered round on an engrossed Jake watching the television, in a semi kind of shock, knowing that it was a serious possibility his dad was in there when the towers collapsed.

"Hi Jakey," Rowena said to Jake in the softest, most gentle voice she could manage.

"Mom," Jake bellowed throwing himself on her, clinging on tight around her neck.

She clasped his waist and reciprocated the love that he was giving her. He also wanted safety, security and to know everything was going to be alright—that his dad would be coming home.

"Is dad with you?" he asked longing for the right answer. "Is he here?"

"No, he's not but I'm sure he won't be long baby," she said, hoping.

"Where is he? He hasn't rung."

"Have you checked the messages?"

"No…I didn't think…," he replied.

Energetically they were already at the answering machine. Physically they were a couple of steps behind. Jake untangled himself from his mom, leapt up and raced downstairs, like he did when he was late for school. Rowena still pretty exhausted was not far behind him.

The light was flashing. There were three messages. Jake pressed play.

"Hi everyone it's Grandma. Matt you okay? I saw the news. I know you're a tough cookie but hope you're doing good. Please ring me. Mom."

"Message Two," the automated machine said.

"Come on, come on." Rowena was impatient.

"Hi it's me." It was Matt.

"Dad!" Jake screamed.

"I couldn't get through on your cell Ro. Listen I'm stuck on the…floor. It's chaos in here. I've…head…up…the roof to try and get airlifted away. I'm sure that'll be fine…and I know I shouldn't say this but just in case…" The line was very crackly and only delivered half a message.

Click. The phone cut off.

Rowena and Jake just looked at each other waiting for the next message.

"Message 3…Hi it's me again I just wanted to say…click." After some more crackling it went dead again.

"Noooooooooooo!" Rowena banged the phone. "Did they airlift anyone to safety Jake? Did they? Did you see it on the news?"

"I didn't see it but it doesn't mean it didn't happen," Jake replied.

"Turn the TV on," she commanded Jake who unusually obeyed. The surround sound of the TV cocooned them in the full scene of downtown Manhattan as helicopters, TV and media crew went bananas scrambling around for the latest news.

"Can you see anyone being lifted?"

"No!"

Rowena flicked frantically through the numerous channels that were normally of no interest to her. Nearly every station was bleeding the news to the nation. Finally something told her to stop.

There was an interview happening in a studio.

"Would you agree with the speculation that no-one above the crash site would have survived?"

"Well it seems unlikely that many people would be able to find a way down but we already have news that some people did miraculously find a route through from above the crash site to the ground floor."

"Do you think people were expecting to be airlifted away to safety?"

"Yes I think this would have crossed the minds of people unable to get down. To go to the next nearest exit point which of course is the roof."

"And why did this not happen," the interviewer quizzed the speculating interviewee.

"Well as you know it was very smoky and explosions from within the towers would still be a possibility. I imagine it would have been more of a risk to try and fly rescue helicopters so close. That is probably why it didn't happen."

Rowena started to sink into herself. She went as white as a sheet, dropped the remote control and just let the words drift over her.

"...But many people I believe were actually evacuated before the collapse. The estimated figures we are getting is that perhaps as many as 6,000 were in there. But obviously we don't know the exact numbers yet."

"If you have a loved one who works at the World Trade Center or someone you know who was supposed to be there then please do not call the police. Please call the help line number appearing on the screen now and the good people at the other end will try and help you."

Jake and Rowena held each other and sobbed. But then suddenly Jake jumped up and grabbed a pen from his bag and on the back of his school book jotted down the digits.

"It might not be too late. He might have changed his mind or got down," he said not wanting to let go of his dad. "Mom, ring this helpline number."

Rowena couldn't really engage for a while so Jake took it upon himself to take control and reached for the phone.

Tom walked in.

"Guess who's got a babe Saturday night?" he said before he noticed the atmosphere.

"Hey you guys what's up?" he said, quite oblivious to what was going on. "You look like some dude just died."

"Have you been on another planet Tom? The twin towers have just collapsed," Jake shouted.

Tom looked like someone had just smacked him in the stomach and knew by the looks on the faces of his mom and brother that this was not a gag.

"What? What about dad? Is he...*dead*?" he asked only wanting to know the answer if it was good news.

"He might be. We dunno yet," Jake said, starting to cry.

"We're trying to find out," Rowena replied, emerging from her trance. "I'll talk to them now Jakey, thanks." She regained control.

Delilah and I just watched, feeling quite helpless because Matt had left his body and there was nothing we could do about it. The laws of the universe could not bring him back. Not physically anyway.

"Matt wants to come back," I told Delilah.

"I think it would help," Delilah responded.

"I'll see you soon," I said as I zipped through the gateway back to the spirit world.

THE EDGE OF TIME

"You know you can't progress, son, until you deal with those issues," I told Matt who looked a little worried about the return-to-Earth tunnel we were about to travel down.

"I know but I don't think I can forgive myself without speaking to my family."

"It's very difficult to communicate to spirits on the Earth when you haven't got a body you know Matt," I said, hoping he wouldn't get his hopes up.

"You managed it."

"Not really," I confessed. "You were in a world of your own most of the time. I'd been trying to get you to leave that job for years."

Matt looked surprised.

"I'm sure when we get back to Earth I'll be able to communicate with Ro, she's very receptive to these things," Matt said positively, not wanting to be defeated.

"That's what Delilah says."

"Who's Delilah?"

"Delilah is Rowena's guide. You'll meet her later."

"Cool," he replied mimicking Jake.

"You ready then?" We were at the front of the line.

"Yeah, of course, let's go." Matt couldn't wait to get back.

I showed the tunnel attendant my pass. After careful scrutiny he said, "Where on Earth do you want to be projected to?"

"New York City."

"I can't put you down anywhere specific right now. The tunnels are jammed. I can only get you to the top of the Statue of Liberty, alright?"

"That'll be fine."

"At what time do you want to go back?"

"What time?" Matt interrupted, sounding shocked. "You mean we could go back before the disaster happens?"

"Yes we could. Time is not linear from this perspective. But there's not much point. You don't want to go through all that again do you?" I checked out.

"No, not if I can't do anything about it," he answered. "But if it could prevent me from dying maybe we should."

"It won't, we can't interfere now."

"Are you two spirits just about ready?" the attendant asked with a smile.

"Sure. 11:00am, September 11th, New York City, top of the Statue of Liberty," I commanded.

Within seconds we were transported down the tunnel, which was like riding the world's largest roller coaster, into the crown of New York's finest lady.

"Wow, what a ride. That was amazing! I feel so alive," Matt screamed as he landed on the Earth plane before he became fully aware of his new environment. "Whoa. It feels so weird, so sticky and heavy."

"In comparison to the spirit world it is," I agreed.

"What happens if we fall off here?" Matt shouted across at me as we both looked over the edge at the long drop down below.

"We'll fly," I said.

"Are you kidding?"

"No, absolutely not. Flying is part of your inheritance. It goes with not having a body anymore."

"Wow." Matt was impressed.

As we turned to the other side of the statue, however, we could see the city being shrouded in ash from the incineration of the twin towers. Looking down there was still much panic and the smoke had formed a large cloud over New York. The metropolis was equipped to save itself ten times over with the services it provided for its people. But it couldn't save everybody this time.

I looked at Matt and saw from his aura he was feeling sad as he looked at the sight that had been his workplace for all those years. All the memories he'd had in that building, good and bad. All the times he wished he could just jump out of the window and fly. Fly away to a better life, a Caribbean island or something other than work and he found it ironic that here he was now about to jump off the side of The Statue of Liberty with his dad and fly back to his family. He just so wanted to be back on the Earth plane again. He was hoping that I knew what I was doing and all his faith lay in me. I knew that I couldn't let him down and that we had to cross the city to get back to his house in Greenwich Village.

"Come on son. Let's go."

We stood on the side of Liberty's crown.

"But how do you do it?" he asked, like a child about to ride his bike for the first time.

"There's nothing to it. Just jump and imagine yourself flying and you will be. Whatever you want to happen, just imagine it," I instructed.

"Imagine it in your mind and it will eventually manifest."
(The Earth Guide Book)

"Okay pop. Whatever you say," he trusted.

I jumped into the air and hovered way above the ground willing Matt to do the same. He followed my route and stood in the same spot looking down on the world. Below him he could see a few small heads and tiny cars. He closed his eyes and counted in his mind. I could hear him.

"1, 2, 3, 4, 5, 6, 7, 8, 9,...10. Let's do it!" he shouted as he threw himself off the statue.

He arrived next to me and just hovered. "Wow, that's amazing!"

There was a three hundred foot drop below us.

It was still very much a complete shock to Matt's psyche that he was dead. Matt had been through such a range of emotions in such a short amount of time. The biggest thing that kept going through his mind was that if he had known the after life would be like this and he'd meet up with me, he might have lived a more spiritual existence.

Matt focused his attention and started to imagine himself next to me, hovering silently.

"You always were a quick learner Matt," I encouraged.

"But how do you move forward?" Matt asked.

"In exactly the same way," I replied. "Just imagine it."

Matt suddenly zoomed off at great speed into the sky towards Ellis Island.

"Hey, hold on, not so fast," I shouted after him.

Matt came to a sudden stop. "Whoops," he said. "I think I got carried away. I didn't realise it would be so easy."

An image of Rowena flashed into his mind and he wondered where she was and what she was doing. He was also concerned about how worried she would be and what he could do to help.

"I just thought about..."

"Rowena, yes, I know," I interrupted.

"Stop reading my thoughts, dad. I'm gonna start feeling paranoid," Matt protested.

"I can't help it. I can feel them. I've been with you for such a long time I'm totally tuned in to what you're thinking."

"Really, that's too scary."

"Most of them were about work though, wouldn't you agree?"

"How do you read them?" Matt enquired not even bothering to answer my question.

"Well, when you go beyond your physical form a thought just becomes like a word," I explained.

"Mmmmm," Matt digested this idea. "So I could read your thoughts then?"

"You already are. This is how we're having this conversation. Not through talking words but through thinking them," I explained.

"I need to find Rowena," Matt suddenly announced. "I need to tell her that I'm okay. I need to see my kids. I know they're used to me being home late but they'll be devastated if they think I'm not coming home at all." Matt's energy started falling rapidly.

"Okay son, don't worry. Just follow me. Stay close. I don't want you getting lost in the shadowlands," I instructed him.

"The what?"

"The shadowlands."

"What's that?"

"I'll explain later."

Matt was curious as to what I meant but trusted my every word and knew my tone of voice meant it was serious.

I pushed my energy upwards and felt myself lift away from the magnetic pull of the Earth and started to fly, like a superhero would, through New York City. Matt stayed just a few feet behind me.

His mind was whirring over and over with exasperation. "I can't believe I'm dead. Well I'm not am I? I'm very much alive—more alive even. I just wish my family were with me. I don't mean I wish they were dead. Maybe I do. It's not that bad. I mean, I wish they knew I was alright and that I could hug them again. I didn't hug them before I died. I wish I'd hugged them. I'll never be able to do that again. Not until they die anyway. I hope they got my text messages. Maybe this is just a dream? I'm gonna wake up soon next to Rowena in our lovely bedroom and I won't go to work."

I beamed a thought back to him. "It's not a dream Matt, it's real. This is real. It's more real than you can ever imagine—much more."

Below us, in this world of illusions, we were passing over traffic and people in deep contemplation and shock trying to escape Manhattan. The behaviour of the city was unusual. The disaster brought out the best in people. Acts of kindness were aplenty with bottles of water being given out by shopkeepers, drivers stopping to offer lifts out of the city, people waiting quietly in line for public telephones, asking strangers what they knew, places of worship inviting individuals in to take refuge. Times Square was one big electronic heart beat as people stood still watching TV screens in silence.

The only escape away from the Trade Center was north or east and for most people this was by foot. Below us this flowing river of bodies were only guessing they would be safer away from Manhattan when, in fact, another plane could have appeared at any time, choosing its target anywhere. Once they realised that the first crash was not an accident the second one must have been the spark that lit the fire of this mass exodus. In shock at the day's events, everyone was wondering if another attack would happen and if, in fact, New York was fast becoming a war zone.

The vibration of fear was emanating from the Earth plane into the astral realm and both Matt and I could feel it as we flew through the thickness of it. The thought forms had created a fog of negativity, a denseness that we had to raise ourselves above. This is similar to how it works

190

on an individual basis. The aura collects thought forms, which can be captured now by something called Kirlian photography, which is an instrument the Russians have developed to photograph the auric field with a special camera. Spirit guides can see these auric formations and know what the predominant feature is of an individual, whether they are healthy or not, what kind of thoughts they are thinking, etc. An individual who is thinking negatively all the time will create an aura of blackness around them. This was happening to New York. But at the same time, however, New York was in some ways at its most positive as the fire fighters selflessly threw themselves into buildings and people bravely looked after one another, risking their own lives. There was no looting and pillaging and taking advantage of the situation. New York was morally firm, mentally wobbling but spiritually alive!

"I feel so sick," Matt was thinking.

"I know. It's the thoughts forming in the astral plane. Just think about someone or something you love," I advised.

"No problem," Matt said, as he focused on Rowena and his boys. The love he'd generated on the Earth plane was bigger than he'd originally thought and he was able to call on it to help him get through the next few moments. His vibration became much lighter and he was able to travel through the denseness with great ease.

"That's it, kid. You're doing it," I reassured him.

Another large astral cloud of negativity was on the horizon and I knew that we had to avoid it as going through it may prove problematic. But it was too late as Matt entered its energetic field ahead of me and I felt his whole astral body starting to seize up with these lower, negative vibrations. He couldn't help but take some of it on board and felt fearful, which caused him to fall.

"Are you alright?" I projected, looking back.

But there was no reply.

"Matt?" I shouted.

There was no sign of Matt now. He had been sucked into this negative astral vortex and was plunging deeper and deeper. I knew I shouldn't have gone through the cloud but Matt seemed so sure he was secure in his vibration. How could he be? He'd only just left his body. He wasn't secure in anything but I just wanted to get him back home as fast as possible. I looked down and saw him swirling into this dark black hole. Without thinking of the consequences for myself I dived after him. Swooping like a bird in pursuit of its prey—focused and determined.

"Matt over here," I shouted to him. "Behind you. Look behind you."

But it was too late. He had lost his bearings and couldn't find himself at all. Like a freefalling skydiver I fell through the sky until I was ahead of him. The magnetic pull of this nauseous energy field was both all-consuming and repelling.

I felt very much on my own and remembered what we had learned in class about dealing with darker, denser energies. "Ask for protection and help" I heard my wise teacher say. So in my moment of desperation I tuned in to Doris, the greatest rescuer of all time, to try and access some of her energy.

Within seconds she was there with me. Her wings spread long and thick and her light shone so bright it was impossible to look at her. Between her and her angelic entourage a net of light was created, made purely of thought beams, which captured Matt as he fell.

"Take him to his family as quickly as possible," she beamed, melting my distress. "Code 101. Teleport yourself right now. I'll help you."

She meant that I had to materialise myself and Matt back to his house without crossing New York City, just by thinking and wishing we were there. This was quite a difficult process to take someone else's energy to another location and guides aren't supposed to do that, unless it is an absolute emergency—a code 101. That's what it says in the manual anyway. This was certainly a 101 emergency.

I closed my eyes and thought about the place in the house Matt was most connected to, his office. Slowly we started disintegrating from the thick smoky sky above Manhattan and within a few minutes these awful images were replaced by sturdy walls covered in charts, a desk with a computer on it, a chair, lamp, familiar red rug and two beautiful photographs of Jake and Tom.

12:00AM

"Matt, Matt, wake up, we're here, we're in your office," I whispered quite forcefully to him.

Matt was coming round. He looked at the charts on the wall, which he recognised, then saw the saying he had put up on the computer which said:

Those who fail to plan, plan to fail.

He sat up with a jolt.

"Thank God for that. I had the most terrible dream," he said. "I dreamt I was at work and the building was struck by planes and my dad appeared and...," he stopped in mid sentence as he turned to see me, large as life, sitting at his desk with the chair swivelled round looking straight at him.

"Oh, Jesus Christ. I'm still in it," he gasped.

"It's not a dream, son. You have died and right now you're on the astral plane of the Earth world, coming back to see your family. Remember?"

Matt looked around and heard Rowena's voice downstairs. He did remember very much. In fact how could he forget? It had been a complete nightmare on one hand and a complete revelation on the other.

"Rowena!" he shouted as he jumped up and went to open the door but couldn't. His hand went straight through it.

"Not this again," he said with frustration. "How do I open this goddamn door?" he yelled.

"Just walk through it Matt," I replied. "Like this."

I demonstrated by merely walking straight into and therefore through it. I popped my head back through and said, "Just don't stop walking otherwise you'll end up in the door itself."

Matt didn't hesitate and leapt through the door falling down the stairs at the other side, landing in a dishevelled heap at the bottom. Picking himself up swiftly he carried on the descent towards his family's voices. He really couldn't get there quickly enough.

Fortunately, the door to the front room was open. Rowena was still holding on to the phone, her tear stained, mascara smudged eyes, full of grief and trauma reflected the events of the day.

Matt ran over and threw his arms around her but she didn't move, didn't flinch, didn't do anything as he passed straight through her and landed near the television on the other side. Even the woman in the phone box had more of a reaction, he thought.

Delilah, who was sitting on the sofa, behind her said, "She can't feel you honey. She's far too distressed for that."

This was an unfamiliar voice to Matt as he turned round quickly to see Delilah's comforting smile.

"Who the hell are you? What you doing in my house?" he demanded.

"Has he learned nothing in his life review?" she quipped.

"He's doing fine," I said in his defence.

"Don't be alarmed. My name is Delilah. I am Rowena's spiritual guide. Nice to meet you, in the astral at last. I'm sorry you've had to go through such trauma, honey," Delilah sympathised.

Matt couldn't take it all on board right now. He looked to his father for reassurance who just nodded, then looked back at Rowena who was still holding the phone.

"What's the point?" Rowena said throwing the phone to the chair unknowingly at Delilah. But not hanging up.

"Hey watch it. After all I've done for you today that's the thanks I get," she joked.

"Rowena, Rowena it's me Matt. It's Matt. I'm here. I'm still alive," Matt cried.

Rowena looked blankly.

"I love you. I love you. I love you. I'm so sorry," he said.

"She can't hear you," Delilah told him.

"I wanna tell her how much I love her," Matt said desperately.

"You can do that but she can't hear you. She will be able to feel you later when she's not in such a state, I'm sure, but not now honey. She won't feel anything now," Delilah counselled him.

Matt started kissing her chaotically. First her hands, then her arms, then her face, then all over, ending up at her feet. He held on to them sobbing.

"No, no, no, no, no, no, no, no, no, no, nooooo," Matt wailed.

After a while he turned his attentions to Jake and Tom who were sitting silently on the sofa, staring into space.

"Jake I love you. I love you. I'm so sorry I shouted at you this morning. I know I haven't been a good dad lately but I'll make it up to you I promise."

"How you gonna do that, you haven't got a body no more?" Delilah reminded him.

Jake started to cry.

"He's dead, I know he is. He's dead!" He got up and stormed out of the room.

"Can he hear me?" Matt asked.

"He can feel you. He's the one most aware of your presence. He's very sensitive," I said.

Matt then tried his eldest son and sat on the sofa next to him, in Jake's empty spot, hugging him.

"I love you too Tom. I'm so sorry. I'm so sorry."

The guilt was starting to surface now. He was realising that there was no way on this Earth that he could make amends. The mistakes he had made with his children had been made. No apologies had been given. It had all been done and the ripples of his actions would be felt through this cause and effect universe. Recently he hadn't even let them know how much he loved them. They didn't even know he loved them and it was too late.

He wondered if they had received the frantic text messages he was trying to send from the top of the south tower and the answering machine messages he'd left. As if that would make a difference, he thought. How could he possibly forgive himself now?

At this moment the door bell rang.

"Who's that?" Rowena and Matt said simultaneously.

It was the next door neighbour, Julie.

"Oh hi Rowena, are you alright? Is everything alright? Is Matt alright? Has he come home?" Julie asked at high speed.

"Oh, Julie, he's not home. He's not home. His message got cut off," Rowena sobbed.

"Oh sweetie, come here." She took a crying Rowena into her arms.

"You don't know for sure. Miracles do happen you know. He might be fine," she said not wanting to be pessimistic. "Where are the kids?"

"They're in there," Rowena replied.

Julie's guide was a small Chinese lady called Toola who was standing beside them.

"Hi Toola," acknowledged Delilah.

"Hi Dee," she bowed.

Matt looked at the situation and the nightmare he was living, or rather not really any more. He made a few more attempts to grab someone's attention, who still had a body but they all came to nothing.

After a while Matt said, "I need to see my mom...and my brother. Maybe I'll have better luck with them."

"We need to teleport ourselves there. We can't cross the city again," I told him. "If we both think of the same spot, say the entrance, we'll get there much more easily."

In an instant both Matt and I were gone. The power of our minds made it so.

12:20AM

Matt and I materialised ourselves into Lennox Hill hospital. The place was not as busy as you might have expected as the casualties from the disaster were few. It was mainly "you got out alive or you didn't", with not much in between, other than eyes being affected by dust, ash and smoke. And most casualties were taken to hospitals nearer the Trade Center.

Inside there were a few shocked souls walking alongside their own bodies that were laid out on stretchers. They were confused and hoping they could get back in somehow, just as I had when I'd died. Matt could see them too.

"These people look awful," he commented, pointing at a woman who had been hit by some flying debris across her head. Her astral body still held the scars although she was not in pain. She was bent over her own body.

"What are the nurses doing around here? Someone should be looking after her. She's got a massive hole in her head," Matt gasped.

"Her body is dead Matt. That's her astral form you're looking at," I replied.

"Then someone should tell her." Matt was feeling concerned. After a few frustrated moments Matt ran across. She didn't even look up at him.

"Hey lady, you've died, you've left your body. You need to go to the other world now," he stated, quite matter of factly.

But there was no response.

"Are you sure she's dead? She's not responding," Matt questioned.

"She can't hear you Matt because she's not had the realisation that she's dead yet. Once she does she'll be able to find the light."

"What if she doesn't realise?"

"She will."

I was pleased Matt was starting to care about others and returning to his true, loving nature. He was always very loving as a young boy.

"We need to find Luke quickly. It looks like it's this way," I said reading the signs.

We glided down the corridors following the directions for the maternity ward.

In Luke and Lorraine's room we found Luke holding Abigail, embarking on her exciting Earthly life, only minutes old this time round but thousands of years old in the universe.

"She's so sweet," Luke gurgled. "She's got your eyes."

"Do you think? I think she's got your nose," Lorraine gurgled back.

Luke hadn't told Lorraine exactly what had happened down at the Trade Center yet just said there had been another terrorist attack and the city was a bit shocked but all was fine.

I sat down in an empty chair and let Matt try and communicate with his brother.

Matt felt odd being a fly on the wall during their precious first birth moments and this was also the first time Matt had seen his brother, in the flesh, since New Year.

"Hey man," Matt tried interrupting. "Hey man, it's me, Matt. Can you hear me? Do you have any latent psychic abilities at all?"

There was nothing from Luke. Everything just continued as normal, like we weren't even there. Matt tried a few more times. He tried tugging his shirt and walking through him but nothing happened. At the back of Luke's mind I knew he was worried about his brother but was also trying not to let it spoil this wonderful moment with his new baby.

"It's no use," Matt complained to me.

Unexpectedly Win opened the door. She had somehow managed to get into the city and flung her arms around her son and daughter-in-law.

"Mom," Luke and Matt said at the same time.

Matt joined in hugging her too.

"Mom, I'm so sorry, I'm sorry, I have been so selfish. Forgive me. Can you hear me?" blurted Matt.

"Can you hear me?" he repeated.

"She will hear you on some level. But psychically she's as deaf as a post," I was sorry to say. "She's not responded to me in the last twenty odd years so I don't think she'll respond to you."

"It's useless. What's the point? I'm dead now. That's it. I'll never be able to communicate with them again. Ever," Matt realised.

September 12th 2001

9:30PM

Almost a day and a half had passed with still no news of Matt. Was he trapped somewhere amongst the rubble? Would he be one of those miracle survivors? They were still finding people. Jake had taken to his bed and there he had been for almost twenty-four hours, not even emerging for food. His drapes were pulled tight and his duvet cover pulled as far over his head as it would go. Jake knew his dad wouldn't be coming home and wanted to bury himself away, not knowing how to deal with the pain. He reminded me of Matt when he was young.

Tom, on the other hand, was more like Rowena, not admitting defeat until it really was all over, and was trying to be optimistic by saying the right things to his mom.

Later that evening Rowena lit some candles, put soft music on and was burning incense in her bedroom. She sat with her eyes closed praying to God or whoever was listening, willing with all her might that Matt be brought back to her somehow. That he'd be found alive. She wanted to see him so much she would have agreed to look after him for the rest of her life, even if he had been crippled. In fact she would have done any deal with anyone to get him back.

Rowena was playing their love songs tape, the one she and Matt always found when they were going to make love, or spend a romantic evening together, in front of the fire. Unfortunately there had not been many of those lately and her insecurities about him loving her, or going off her, kept surfacing. She didn't know whether he did still fancy her or not. Matt hadn't indicated any interest for a while now. She knew he'd gotten drunk at an office party and had a sexual encounter with some woman from a higher floor then had an affair with her and was glad she knew. The whole episode had left its scars. It still hurt when she thought about it. But at least there were no secrets and lies between them now. The thoughts were about the other woman and whether she'd survived. She wasn't sure she wanted her to or not. If she'd died did that mean she and Matt could, somehow, be bonded by their death? Rowena didn't like that idea. Strange thoughts whizzed through her mind for quite some time. Soon Ro started wondering what life would be like without Matt but not for long, as she couldn't contemplate living her life without him beside her. This wasn't an option for her right now.

As Rowena sat on her bed there were a thousand questions she wanted to ask Matt. Round and round and round her head they went, making her dizzy, making her feel nauseous. But the burning question in her mind was "do you and did you love me?".

Matt was lying on the bed in his usual position, the left-hand side. His nicotine craving was nagging away at him because he was close to the Earth again. He was aware of Rowena's feelings but not her thoughts at this stage as he hadn't tuned his vibration in enough to reach the wavelength of thought forms from still embodied spirits, even though she was his wife. But it didn't take Einstein to figure out she was devastatingly sad. As she laid out his clothes she smelled them, trying to breathe him back into her life and soul.

"She's wondering whether you really loved her or not?" I told Matt.

Then bang!—a realisation hit Matt, hard—that she loved him so much and she showed it in all her actions toward him, even trying to rescue the relationship with counselling just after New Year, after the affair he'd tried to forget but couldn't. She was a fabulous caring mother and wife. And what was he? A complete bastard, or so he thought. He hadn't done anything for Ro for ages. He didn't deserve her. Why did she stay with him? Why did she love him so much? And then the emotions welled in him, the feelings that had been absent for so many months, the feelings of love for her. Waves cascaded through his energetic body as he lay there watching her.

"I do love you, yes I do, I love you, I did, I do, I will forever. You are the love of my life," he cried.

Rowena remained oblivious to him, tears rolled down her cheeks. She wiped them away with one of his favourite shirts. It was hard for him to witness and so hard for her to feel, so hard. There was still a small glimmer of hope in her heart but this flame was being slowly extinguished as time went by with no real news of him.

Matt turned and looked at me. I was sitting quietly in the corner on Rowena's favourite rocking chair they'd bought at an auction ten years ago, that she used to rock the boys to sleep on.

"Dad, I can't bear it," Matt said wanting it to stop.

"I know son, it's hard. There's no way out, only through it, but it will heal. It will," I reassured him.

I remembered scenes of my own death and the trauma surrounding it all. The ambulance, the hospital, my family's pain. Standing on the edge of the other world waiting to cross, with fear and excitement and in trepidation as to what I might find. Wondering where the next part of my adventure would take me. I could see the light swirling above me just waiting and in the end it was my dog, Jasper, who led the way. My ever faithful companion turned up at the gate between heaven and Earth to reassure me that it was okay. I thought I would never see him again. How wrong I was. Animals have souls too you know and should be treated just like people, with kindness and respect. I wept tears of joy at our reunion. But then on visiting the Earth plane again, only a few hours later, I wept tears of grief. It was such a strong feeling that as one door closes another one opens and these are the biggest, most solid doors any of us will ever have to open and close. Ever.

Right now Matt had his metaphorical foot in the door. But he would make the complete transition and let go of the Earth plane when he was ready, and if I could help him in any way I would. Knowing that we have angels on our side really helps.

"She's in so much pain. What can I do?" Matt asked.

"Just send her love," I replied.

"I am, I am. It's not helping," he panicked.

"It will be Matt, it will be." I tried to reassure him.

"She needs to know that I'm dead. To put her out of her misery," Matt said to both me and Delilah.

"She needs to know you've left your body and you're still alive!" I said.

"She knows," Delilah told us.

"How does she know?" Matt was looking for answers.

"We all know everything on one level, honey," Delilah educated. "My Rowena has been preparing for this event and the loss of you for quite some time. She knew it was coming. This is a big test for her soul."

"But how did she know?"

"Most people, when they are sleeping are able to project themselves into the future. This is done by crossing the three-dimensional barriers that hold time. They can then see what is going to happen to them and use this information subconsciously to prepare for a negative event or divert themselves away from it. This is what Rowena did," I explained.

"No kidding."

"And there's more than that Matt, honey, much more. It will be one of her greatest life lessons too and she'll grow enormously from this," Delilah said being very philosophical.

"There's far more to this world and the journey we make called "life" than we can ever begin to imagine," she added. "And you will find out even more when you return home again."

Our conversation was interrupted by the ring of a fluffy pink phone by the side of the bed.

"Hello, is that Mrs Moretti?"

"Yes," Rowena answered.

"My name is Chris. I'm ringing about your husband Matt," he said solemnly.

"Yes!" There was enthusiasm in her voice. Had they found him? Was he alive by some incredible act of God? Was he?

"We have a body here that has been recovered from the wreckage at ground zero that matches the description you have given of your husband," he relayed.

Rowena's heart sank. "Oh."

"His body is fairly bruised and cut but he was still fully clothed and he had a book in his pocket, which miraculously remained intact. It has your name and number in it," he told her.

That was it then. That was the confirmation. He was dead, she thought.

"But just to make double sure Mrs Moretti we would like you to come down and identify the body. We can show you the actual body, as cleaned up as possible, or we can just show you pictures," he continued.

Rowena had sat down on the side of the armchair with her mouth open. She didn't know what to say. Although she kinda felt it was not over until someone officially said "yes, we have your husband's body", she was still in shock. There was no question about going to see it. She wanted to see it. She wanted to see him. She wanted to be close to him again. Maybe this would help.

We all listened to the conversation and Delilah tried to persuade her to just look at the pictures by putting thoughts in her mind but Rowena's stubbornness won out. She wanted to know for sure that he was dead. She wanted to see his body, in the flesh, dead or not. And nothing would stand in her way!

September 13th 2001

8:00AM

Sitting in the waiting area at the morgue the next day Rowena could barely function. She now hadn't slept for over forty-eight hours and this continual nightmare was the worst experience of her life, by far. The emotional pain she was feeling, in her heart and solar plexus, was ten times worse than labour pains and didn't seem to be getting any better. At least with labour pains she knew it would stop and there was a bundle of joy waiting at the end of it all. But with this pain, however, she had no idea when or if it would ever end.

Delilah was doing all the reassuring things by sending calming messages, telling her it would get better, that she would get through it but unfortunately, often when someone needs to hear the messages the most, this is when they are least receptive. Always a challenge to a guardian angel.

On reception was a lovely woman attending to everybody's needs but Rowena wanted minimum contact. She had been told to wait before she went through to the viewing room.

Matt, myself and Delilah were alongside her. Matt was curious to see his body too. Both Delilah and I knew that it wouldn't be a pleasant experience. It's like seeing a carcass and the question you always have to ask yourself is do you really want your final memory of a person's body, whether it is yours or not, to be of it lying there laid out, stiff and lifeless—an empty vessel.

"I wanna see a dead body," Matt said. "I've never seen one."

"I can understand that, but do you really want to see your own? It'll be a shock," I replied.

"I think I can handle it," he said.

"It's just through here ma'am." The receptionist led the way.

As Rowena followed her into the viewing room Matt followed another lady, who was going to get his body, behind a red curtain and through two swinging doors. I followed him knowing that he still might need my protection. Inside this room were racks of drawers, like filing cabinets, each one containing the final document of someone's life.

She knew exactly which drawer to go to by the clipboard she was carrying.

The energy in the morgue was gross and I couldn't bear it for long and neither could Matt.

"Uuuurghh, I feel awful in here...really sick and...uurgh," Matt said trying to hold on to his energy.

"Come on Matt. Let's go back. There's no point being sucked in," I said. Matt didn't need much persuading, after his experience of the negative forces in the sky over Manhattan a few days ago, so we speedily threw ourselves back through the doors to the viewing room.

"You sure you wanna see ma'am? We could just show you pictures," we heard the receptionist tell Rowena.

"Yeah, I'm sure," Rowena said being brave, not knowing how disfigured Matt's body would be.

Rowena was pacing up and down with nervous anticipation wondering whether, if it was Matt's body, it would be at all recognisable.

There was a distinguishing mark on his left arm she was going to check out and one on his neck. The mark on his arm was a formation of freckles that created a diamond shape if you joined up the dots like a dot to dot.

Rowena had lain on her side stroking his strong, hairy arms joining up the dots with her fingers many times. The other mark on the join of his neck and shoulder looked like a brown bullet wound that had gone splat. Some crazy woman on holiday one year, who claimed she was psychic, told Matt that it was a past life wound. That he had been shot there in a previous incarnation and he was still holding the memory of it. Matt, of course, thought this was the biggest load of nonsense he had ever heard.

But now as he stood there thinking about it he wondered whether there was any truth in it. He hadn't believed in life after death but he was wrong about that. Maybe he had had past lives.

"You have son, but you won't find out about them until we get back and even then it might be a while before you do, if at all. It may not be necessary for you to know," I said. "And you can't believe everything psychics say anyway. Some of it is a load of nonsense. That was probably just a birthmark."

We could hear the body being brought in.

Rowena held her breath and her stomach in at the same time, totally unconsciously. This was the moment of truth which would end her questioning. She paused briefly, wondering whether she really did want to see but she had come too far now not to take the next step.

"Okay, I'm ready," she said to the lady.

The curtain was pulled back.

Rowena looked down and saw Matt's dead face looking up at her. Empty. Rigid. She knew it was his body. A face she had looked at for years. But not like this. Not lifeless like this. His spirit was not there. She knew that he was not there. He must be somewhere else. The energy of this man she loved couldn't just disappear into nothingness. It was at this moment she knew Matt was dead but at the same time knew he was very much alive somewhere else.

"That's not my body." Matt was shocked.

"It is," I replied.

"I look dreadful," he observed.

"What do you expect? It's dead!" I said.

"How come my face isn't burnt or bruised?" Matt asked me.

"Your body must have been trapped in an air pocket or something like that. You'll find this hard to believe but some people survived the whole collapse with only a few scratches." I'd heard.

"No way!"

"Yep, it wasn't their time to die obviously," I commented. "They must have things to complete."

The lady from the back room appeared through the doors with a plastic bag.

"I'm so sorry Mrs Jenkins. Here are his belongings," she said handing the bag to Rowena.

"Look! **The Earth Guide Book** is in there. I can see it," Matt yelled getting excited. "It still looks as good as new."

"That's because it's not from the physical world, therefore its molecular structure is different, keeping it intact," I replied, pleased about its recovery.

"She'll get my message," Matt remembered.

Rowena was curious and took the pocket-sized book from the top of the bag.

"**The Earth Guide Book**? I don't know where on Earth he got this from," she quizzed, quickly putting it back.

"Don't do that. Pick it back up. Open it," Matt yelled again.

But she couldn't hear him so she didn't.

8:45AM

The final twist of the knife had been made and as she drove she couldn't help but look up at the skyscrapers of New York and remember the horror of Tuesday morning. She remembered seeing people throwing themselves out of the building to bring their suffering to an end and she too now thought about throwing herself off one of these tall buildings. There were certainly enough to choose from.

Matt was sitting by her and saw Delilah's quick reaction which made him jump.

"No, you don't wanna do that honey. That wouldn't solve anything," Delilah said to Rowena firmly.

"What's she talking about?" Matt asked me knowing Delilah was working very intensely with his wife.

"Rowena is thinking about throwing herself off The Empire State Building," I replied.

"What? She can't do that!" Matt exclaimed.

"Well she can. She can do whatever she likes. We all have free will remember," I reiterated.

"So she might throw herself off The Empire State?" Matt clarified.

"She might," I said truthfully.

"She won't," Delilah interrupted.

"You didn't think she'd get in that elevator after the dream you gave her but she did," I reminded her.

"*You* influenced her dreams?" Matt was surprised.

"Yes, honey. It takes great skill to get your Earth friend to accept your images into their dreams." Delilah was proud of her achievement.

As she drove, Matt could tell by the comments Delilah was making that Rowena was still thinking about taking her own life.

"She won't do it. It's not in her character. She wouldn't leave the boys," Matt said.

"How do you know Matt? Thousands of people do it every day and thousands more think about doing it," I responded. "Suicide on the Earth plane is an epidemic."

"Well what would happen if she did?"

"In terms of her own evolution and development it would be a real backward step for her and as you know the pain doesn't go away just because you leave your body. She would still have to deal with it, plus there would be all the new pain that would be caused. The guilt, the grief of death itself, losing her children, not completing her life. It's a really, really bad idea."

"Sounds like it!"

"The regret she would have would far outweigh the pain she has now."

"If she did it would I be able to see her?" Matt asked thinking about the possibility of reconnecting with her again.

"By taking your own life you cut yourself off for a time from your loved ones in the spirit world because your spirit is not ready for the next stage and has to almost play catch up with itself to move on. So you would see her eventually. When? I'm not sure," I explained.

"But what about those desperate people who threw themselves out of the towers, like I nearly did?" Matt quizzed.

"There are always exceptional cases. In this case it is not classed as suicide as the body was going to die anyway. The soul just decided to take a different route to it."

Rowena switched the sound system on to distract her mind from all her negative thoughts and the self-help tape came on. "All is well. You are in the right place at the right time," the voice said. She pushed the eject button, rolled down the window and threw it out onto the sidewalk.

"I don't believe you," she screamed. "It's lies. All lies."

She looked across at the subway station.

"You wouldn't wanna do that either," Delilah said to her.

"What's she thinking?" asked Matt.

"About throwing herself in front of a train," Delilah replied.

"Jeeze. I thought she was stronger than this," Matt said.

"Don't underestimate the strength of emotional pain and how much people want it to stop," Delilah said.

"I didn't know she loved me that much?"

"This is not about love Matt. It's about grief. It's about loss of a life, loss of you, loss of a future, loss of dreams, hopes and desires. She thinks she can never be happy again but she can be. Taking your own life is about escape. Escaping from pain, but the irony is you don't."

"She needs to know I'm not dead. That would help."

"Yes it would help," I replied knowing Matt was absolutely right. Knowledge helps everyone live their life.

"You bastards!" Rowena suddenly screeched at the top of her voice making us all jump.

"You bassstarrrds!" she screamed again. "You f****** bastards! You killed my husband."

"She's furious with the hijackers but there will come a point in her own evolution when she will have to forgive them in order to move on," I explained to Matt.

"Forgiveness isn't easy though is it?" Matt replied.

**"Forgiveness is as easy or as difficult as you make it.
It only takes a second to let go and forgive."**

I quoted **The Earth Guide Book** to Matt.

The traffic lights were on go and Rowena now stared into space unaware that they had changed until enough beeps and yells from behind caused her to move. The remainder of the drive back was complete oblivion. If it hadn't been for Delilah taking partial control of her mental functions she might have crashed the car on several occasions.

9:30AM

Back at the house all the curtains were still drawn. Tom was in bed. So was Jake. Rowena knew she had to break the expected news to the boys and that it would be hard for all of them.

By force of habit only she switched the kettle on. She didn't even know if she wanted a drink or not. Neither could she eat and hadn't managed much for days. Her spaced out gaze landed on the knives set, sitting on the side in their wooden holder. A wedding gift from years ago.

"What's she thinking?" Matt asked Delilah worried about her intentions. "Why is she looking at the knives?"

"She's not thinking anything. Her mind is numb," Delilah replied.

We all followed her through the house, up the stairs, into the bathroom. She caught a reflection of herself in the mirror and didn't even care what a mess she looked. She didn't care about anything anymore. All the things she had ever worried about suddenly became so incredibly trivial. Why had she ever thought any of them were worth worrying about?

In the cabinet on the wall Matt's pills and potions jumped out at her. She picked them up one by one and read the labels then put them down on the wooden dresser next to the sink.

"What's she gonna do with those?" Matt panicked.

"I don't know." I looked at Delilah for an answer.

"These would do it," Rowena thought. "They're bound to kill me."

"Not a good idea, honey," Delilah said.

"Is she thinking about swallowing all those drugs?" asked Matt.

"That's what's in her mind," Delilah confirmed.

"Rowena, don't. Rowena, I'm not dead. I'm still here. I'm here and I love you," Matt said to an oblivious Rowena who was sitting on the toilet looking at the pills just thinking about Matt. Wanting to be close to him and wondering whether by finishing her life too she would be.

"That's not a good idea," Delilah repeated, which worried Matt even more.

"Why can't you just appear to her? You're her guardian angel aren't you? I thought you could do amazing things," Matt pressed Delilah.

"I could but I don't think she'll do it," she replied.

"But what about free will?" Matt shouted.

"She has constraints within her free will," Delilah said.

"What you talking about?" He was still shouting.

"Rowena's mental and spiritual development will stop her from cutting her Earthly life short. This development will hinder her free will," Delilah said very seriously.

The Earth Guide Book says:

> **"Free will exists but only within certain limits.**
> **A soul who is further along in their spiritual**
> **development will have less control over their free will."**

It also says:

> **"Souls who have decided to return to Earth for a specific purpose**
> **will experience limited free will so they can carry out their task."**

Their conversation was cut short as Rowena swept all of Matt's pills and potions off the side of the dresser and into the bin.

As she was about to clean herself up she had the thought to empty the plastic bag full of Matt's belongings on to the floor and on doing this she couldn't help but notice **The Earth Guide Book.**

"Look, look, she's found the book," Matt cried.

"Think of a problem, open the book and there will be your answer," she said opening it to the page Matt had written his message on, which first of all said,

"Love survives death and can act as a bridge between two souls."

And underneath this he'd written,

Dear Ro,

I am now only one floor down from heaven and hoping there really is one and they'll let me in if I die! I write this in the hope that if I don't make it out of here somehow this book will survive and be returned to you. I want you to know that I love you so much. Thank you for everything you have ever done for me. I know I didn't deserve you. I'm sorry I wasn't better. Please tell the boys that I love them too.

You are simply the best, forever yours

Matt xxx

Her heart ached with longing.

But on reading the message it gave her the words and the energy she needed to drag herself out of her downward spiralling pit of suicidal thoughts. She washed her face and left the bathroom to tell her two precious sons that their dad's body had been found, he wouldn't be coming home but he did leave a message for them.

This time it was Matt's turn to cry.

Two weeks later

10:30AM

The pews were packed with well-wishers. Several of Matt's work colleagues were there, including Stuart and Carla, who had not made it to work on September 11th. There were friends and relatives from both sides and people who had just wandered in and wanted to give their condolences to the other victims of the disaster, those left behind.

The church was splattered with flowers—lilies, roses, carnations, sunflowers. All sorts. Matt didn't really have a preference and Rowena couldn't decide. She thought that having to deal with someone's funeral, especially the one you love the most in the world, so soon, when grief is riding high, was unfair. The rules people had made up about burying the dead quickly seemed odd.

The reason people do get on with it quickly is because dead people usually like to hang around to see their funerals and it is only after the major grieving has been done that dead friends or relatives feel free to go, to pass over.

Matt was walking up and down the aisle looking around at the gathering and wondering who had turned up and who had not. He was pleasantly surprised by the turn out, even his Uncle Jack was there. This surprised him as he couldn't stand his Uncle Jack and he thought the feelings were pretty mutual.

"Never assume to know what another is thinking about you. What others think is of no real consequence. Just concentrate on your own loving thoughts."

Matt read in my **Earth Guide Book**. But Uncle Jack for God's sake, Matt still thought.

"Why do people wear black at funerals? It's so dull and gloomy," Matt asked as he watched all the black suits and black dresses stroll into church.

"Funerals are sad generally because people don't realise that death is not a final curtain but a mere walkway into a new place, a new adventure. As you now know, in our world we celebrate when a soul comes home and we're sad when they leave," I replied.

"I'm starting to look forward to going back now," Matt remembered.

"Good, you must be clearing some of your emotion here. That will save you having to do it over there," I praised.

It wouldn't be long after the funeral that Matt would decide to leave the Earth plane forever. In the spirit world there are many different spheres that offer different opportunities for growth and learning.

The organist took his seat precariously at the keyboard. Although he had played at a hundred funerals he always felt the pressure of getting it right. Fingers poised, keyboard waiting, he plunged into the chords of the funeral march. The most unhappy tune you could ever dare to imagine.

"That's cheery," Matt said to him, watching him play.

The hearse arrived. It slowly pulled into the driveway followed by the entourage of people who were upset to see Matt go. His family were mourning the loss of a father, husband and friend. Rowena stepped out of the black vehicle wearing a large black hat with a see-through veil to hide her tears. Tom and Jake were behind looking sombre and smart. There were no words to describe what was happening in their hearts. Grief is a very painful emotion. It's like a part of you dies as we have to detach and let go. Dreams and futures are shattered in an instant when somebody dies and a new reality has to be created.

Rowena, Jake and Tom made their way through the church to sit by Rowena's mum and dad, Win, brother, sister-in law, new baby. They were all on the front pew looking incredibly grim but holding it together for the sake of, well, God knows what. Why bother holding it together at a funeral? That's the time to grieve.

"I'm still alive everyone," Matt said brushing passed them. Matt ran up and down the aisle shouting, "I'm alive. I'm alive. I'm totally alive and I don't have to go to work." Jake went shivery again which made Matt stop and attempt more communication with him.

"Jake, I love you Jake, I'm still here I'm not dead," Matt said to a rigid looking Jake. Jake shook himself thinking he was imagining it all.

"You're not imagining me Jake. I'm still here. Can you feel me?" he quizzed his youngest son.

"Dad is that you?" Jake responded in his head. Matt could hear Jake's thoughts too.

"Yeah. You can hear me?" he asked.

"I think so but I may be going mad," Jake replied.

Matt turned to me and said, "He can hear me, Jake can hear me! And I can hear him!"

I was pleased for Matt, he'd made a breakthrough.

"You're not going mad Jake," Matt said which really freaked Jake out.

I just nodded. I knew Jake had the potential to develop his psychic side. It could be a very strong gift for him in the future if he chose it.

"On Earth people are guided down one path or another, according to what they need to experience but ultimately it is their choice. People can choose to go with the flow or against it."
(The Earth Guide Book)

Matt had gone against the tide for quite some time during his life, as he had disconnected from the source, others call God, The Great Spirit, a higher self but it was ultimately from himself.

"I love you Jakey," Matt repeated.

"I love you too dad," he replied.

"Tell your mom that I love her too, will you?"

Jake ignored this and responded with, "Dad, where are you? What you doing? I know you're not in that box."

The coffin was slowly floating down the aisle carried by four burly men.

"I'm just hanging around here for a while. I'm a spirit now, well I always was apparently but now I'm even more of one because I don't have a body, which is not that good for me and you but at least I'm not dead and you can hear me," he blurted.

Jake had switched off as he looked at the coffin and saw the picture of his dad on the side. His mum was crying, wiping away her tears with one of Matt's old handkerchiefs. The burning feeling in Jake's chest that he'd been keeping under tight lock and key pushed through in a big burst and he wept for the loss of his dad, devastated that he would never see him again.

"I can't believe I'll never see him again," he thought.

"You will," Matt said to him. "When you die you'll see me again like I saw my dad again. You will."

But Jake was too emotional now to hear Matt's reassuring attempts. The funeral continued in the usual sombre way.

As the hymns were sung Rowena started to shuffle with anxiety as she mentally prepared herself to recite the poem she'd written. Matt's favourite hymns weren't amongst them as they were *Glad That I Live Am I* and *All Things Bright and Beautiful*. Rowena thought that they wouldn't be appropriate but Louis Armstrong did feature heavily, as he was Matt's ultimate music hero.

From the pulpit the sea of people looked warm and friendly. Energetically nearly all of them were pushing out pink streams of light towards Rowena, a sign of unconditional love. Matt saw some people had heavy dark clouds around their heads and figured it was bad lifestyle or thoughts or radiation or a combination of them all. He was right.

She recited her poem.

"You were the petals of my rose.

The captain of my ship.

The silver lining of my cloud

The one who made me laugh and smile.

You were the guardian of my day

The safe keeper of my night.

The sea that met my shore

But now you are no more."

She sobbed.

Matt was moved. He brushed his cheeks and felt tears. He didn't understand how he could feel tears without a body. The energy in his heart charka area (his chest) was full of love. He had never experienced such full love in all his life. This was an alien feeling to him and one that he wished he had felt before whilst on Earth. Matt had cut himself off from his own love energy by burying himself in the trivialities of the world. Stocks, shares, insurances, performances, occupied his mind most of the time, most of the day and night.

What Matt didn't understand was that whatever is in your mind creates your life experience. The old saying "you are what you think" is so true.

"Whatever you focus on becomes your world."
(The Earth Guide Book)

Matt was starting to feel regretful. How could he have missed the opportunity on Earth to learn how to love? Rowena hadn't. She was always working on loving him. He even cheated on her. Why did she love him? She didn't deserve him. She deserved much better.

The agony of people standing up and telling others how much they loved Matt and listing his good qualities, not surprisingly, soon became too much for him to bear. This was not the Matt he knew. Matt was now falling into the depths of low self-esteem. The more good things people said the worse he felt. "I've fooled them all," he thought to himself.

Before the funeral had properly finished Matt headed towards the door. He couldn't take anymore. I followed him. He sat on the wall outside desperate for a cigarette.

"I'm desperate for a smoke?" he said wonderingly.

"Being between worlds the memory of your Earth life is still pulsating in your astral body causing the nicotine craving. Your emotional state is feeding that craving. If you release your emotions Matt and become at peace with yourself you won't want one and once we return to the spirit world again the craving will just disappear," I explained.

"I can't stand it anymore," he said. "I can't freakin' stand it."

"What can't you stand?" I asked.

"All those nice things they're saying about me. If only they knew what an idiot I've been."

"Matt all those things are true. You *are* a good person and we all make mistakes sometimes," I tried to reassure him. "If you were perfect you wouldn't have been on Earth you'd have been in the angelic realms somewhere with little wings." I tried to lighten his energy which was feeling heavier and heavier.

"But look at my life pop. You saw it. All those times I've been such a bad husband to Ro, who didn't deserve it. Look at her she's an absolute angel. And to my kids. I've been such a useless father. But the worst thing is I knew I was but didn't do anything about it."

"Well that's a good realisation to have Matt," I responded.

"No it's not. I feel terrible," he replied.

226

"But once you realise the truth about yourself, Matt, you can change things."

"How can I change things now I'm dead?"

"As you said earlier, you need to talk to your family so you can complete and move on," I encouraged him.

"How am I gonna do that? I've been trying. They can't hear me." Matt was desperate.

Two Months Later

7:00PM

One of the ways for a human to receive a message from the spirit world is through a spiritual medium. A medium is someone who uses their own body as an instrument to communicate from the deceased to the living.

Delilah had heard through the spirit grapevine that there was someone who was very capable demonstrating at a venue in Soho on November 22nd.

Delilah wasted no time in guiding Rowena to her, using all the tricks of the spirit guide trade. She'd read **The Earth Guide Book** a million times already and almost wished she could go back and have another life so she could practice some of the things she'd learned.

The venue was packed. Many people gathered to hear news of their loved ones hoping they would get a message or some confirmation of life after death.

"They here yet?" Matt asked me.

I looked into the room, psychically scanning it for their energies but picked up nothing.

"No, can't see them," I replied.

I noticed a few familiar faces. Brad's wife and children were there including Laura, Tom's new girlfriend, sitting at the back looking very miserable. Stuart had arrived with his wife. He hadn't had a diabetes-related episode since September 11th and thought it was all very odd. Patrick was also there with his boyfriend. Patrick had turned highly religious since the day, now universally remembered as Nine-Eleven, and thanked God on a regular basis for giving him the sack.

"Let me see," Matt said doing the same thing as I had done, scanning the room remotely. I'd taught him everything he knew, of course.

He recognised the girl from the top of the tower sitting there with, he presumed, her mom, who was linking her arm tightly like an over-protective parent. "How the hell did she get out?" Matt wondered.

Back stage Annie was being prepared by her guardian angel who acted as a gatekeeper to stop unwanted spirits from entering the space. There are spirits that do want to just have a good old chat with anyone and can jump into an untrained medium's body. But that's another story. Annie's body was alive and tuned in to the right frequency of the spirit world.

Matt was feeling incredibly nervous about the night. So many times in his life he had said the wrong things. He didn't want to do or say the wrong thing now. He couldn't afford to get it wrong and he hoped the medium was as good as rumour made her out to be.

"They're here, they're here," Matt said, as he saw Rowena open the door of the hall. She looked so beautiful he wished he could have his body back, even if it was for just one more night, so he could hold her in his arms all night. His heart ached when he saw her. He wanted to make everything alright and God he'd do it so differently this time. But he knew he didn't have another chance. He'd had it.

**"Life is not a dress rehearsal. You may get to live
other lives but you only get to live this life once."
(The Earth Guide Book)**

This made him feel very sad and even more anxious about getting it right tonight.

Rowena led the way followed closely by Jake and Tom. Behind them was Win. Win had hidden Misty under her coat and her little nose popped out as she sniffed around. They walked along the back of the hall squeezing passed people to get to the far corner where there were just a few seats left.

"Do you think dad's met Elvis?" Jake asked Tom as they sat down.

"Probably not," Tom replied. "I hope he's met Marilyn Monroe."

"Yeah, cool but I doubt it," said Jake.

Rowena smiled inside to herself at their banter.

"They might as well be in Texas, sitting all that way over there. Can't they get any closer?" Matt wondered still able to overhear their conversation, however, by pushing his energy closer.

"Don't worry Matt they could be at the other side of the world and they'd still get your messages. Time and space don't really exist on a spiritual level," I said.

Annie wasn't planning on going into full trance, i.e. being taken over completely by a spirit, that evening and nor did Matt want to occupy her body. He knew what the sensation was like after the experience with the cab driver downtown and wasn't sure he wanted that again. Although being in Annie's body would be very different as she kept it as pure and as vibrant as possible.

In Annie's dressing room, which was just a little room at the back of the hall, the light was starting to descend and her spirit guide, who overshadowed her body to help get the messages across to people, was preparing Annie to face the audience.

As her door opened a sudden hush descended, followed by a few murmurs echoing around the room, "she's here", "that's her", "look", "it's starting".

Annie glowed from head to toe. Dressed in a purple dress with a white shawl over her shoulders she gracefully took to the stage. Eyeing the audience she drank in her surroundings knowing that many people were there tonight desperate to heal.

"Good evening," she said. "Thank you for coming out tonight on such a cold night."

A few people replied. Others shuffled uncomfortably on their seats not knowing what to expect as this was their first time at a spiritual meeting.

"For those of you who don't know me my name is Annie and if you're new to this game, then welcome. We're gonna have a reunion party tonight. There are a lot of spirits here that passed over on that fateful day of September 11th and I hope we can reconnect them to their friends and families tonight."

Tears were falling already around the room but Rowena held hers back with a strained gulp.

"I'm being drawn to the young lady in the middle of the row here with the pink top on," she said immediately tuning in and wasting no time.

"Me?" a young woman replied pointing at herself.

It was the cell phone girl from the top of the tower.

"Yes, you, angel," Annie confirmed. "You were in the building weren't you? But you escaped just before it collapsed. You ran and ran and ran, not believing your luck didn't you?"

"Yeah," she nodded.

"You'd almost resigned yourself to dying," Annie asserted.

Another nod.

"Then you had the thought to try a different stairwell and it was clear."

This was exactly right. She had found a way down over on the south side of the building which was unobstructed, she was thinking.

"Well, you sat at the top of that tower and used a phone that was not yours and then you had guidance to move…" She nodded. "This guidance, angel, came from your sister, who calls herself Jo, Josie…something like that."

"Jodie," she shouted.

The skeptics in the audience were amazed. The girl's mother had her handkerchief out and was wiping her eyes.

"She died when you were only seven and she was nine. She wants you to know that you're never alone and that she loves you…and she loves you too," Annie said directing the last part of the message to her mom.

The spirit of the girl was directed away from Annie's aura by a guide as her message was complete. She felt elated she could tell her sister that she was still with her.

"Why didn't you direct *me* down that stairwell?" Matt said to me sounding a little cross.

"Your higher self had decided to die that day Matt. I was just helping you have a good ending and get across quickly," I replied.

"Is it my turn now?"

"No, not yet," I said, as a tall well built figure took his place by Annie.

"Jesus Christ," Matt said suddenly falling backwards.

"What's up?" I asked.

"It's that guy," he said shocked.

"What guy?" I looked.

"The guy that tried to kill me. Were you with me that night? You must have been?" Matt asked.

"The five hundred dollar eyeglasses night?" I thought he was referring to.

"Yeah, that night."

"Of course, I was always with you when you were in danger."

"Yeah, it was you putting those crazy thoughts into my head wasn't it?" Matt grinned.

"No you were quite capable of thinking those things on your own. You have a sharp mind," I replied. "Just because guides can influence thoughts and put messages into our Earth friend's minds, it doesn't mean we do it all the time. What would be the point in that? Then we might as well have taken their body and lived their life instead. It kinda defeats the object."

"That guy, I swear to God, dad, is about to talk to some dude here," Matt whispered.

Annie looked around the room feeling for the right person.

"Who's he gonna to talk to?" Matt was intrigued.

"We're about to find out."

"I don't think I can do this with him here."

"Don't be stupid. He can't kill you now, you're already dead," I assured him.

"Yeah I suppose that's one good thing," Matt said. "But his energy is all creepy and awful."

"Don't worry he can't harm you."

"I'm being drawn to you madam, in the middle, with the white coat on." Annie pointed.

"I don't believe it, it's…" Matt stood with his astral jaw gaping. "It's… Tracey. She survived. She was behind me and Brad on the train that morning. Why is he talking to *her*?"

"I'm picking up a male friend of yours. He's very attractive. He says to say the name Ross, Russ and he's showing me a red pick up truck. Does this mean anything to you?"

She nodded.

"He doesn't want to say much except he's sorry he couldn't handle his aggression," Annie told Tracey.

Then suddenly it all made sense. Matt's mind flashed back to Tracey's declaration of freedom and the bruises he saw on her body. He remembered his words in the bar. Matt thought his stalker had got the wrong guy, but in fact, he might have been sleeping with his girlfriend.

"I thought he was just a weird psycho. Tracey told me she didn't wanna go back to Russ. He must be Russ. He must've found out about us and wanted me dead," Matt transmitted to me.

"But he's sorting himself out now over there. He's getting help. He's much better."

Tracey nodded again.

"I hope so," Matt said.

He didn't hang around long and moved away from the medium's auric field pretty swiftly.

"It's you now son."

As Russ walked away Matt had to walk forward which meant that their paths would cross. As they did Matt looked at Russ who recognised him. Russ smiled at him. A gesture that said "no hard feelings pal" and Matt attempted a smile back. This small interaction healed the events that happened on the Earth plane in an instant and it was indeed divine timing as it freed up some of Matt's nervousness to concentrate on the next mammoth task.

"I'm over here at the back now," Annie said. "Yeah the family at the back."

"Please tell my two sons that I haven't met Elvis yet," Matt started.

"This man I'm talking to is your dad and he says that he hasn't met Elvis yet."

The audience laughed and Jake and Tom looked at each other as if to say "cool" but the outburst of emotion Rowena had tried so hard to squash down couldn't be contained any longer. She burst into tears.

Matt was also upset. You may not think it possible but in the spirit world we have emotions and can cry, in a slightly different way than on Earth but a way that you will experience one day.

"On the day I died she came to the south tower with my briefcase but never made it up to my floor," Matt explained to Annie.

"I'm getting the image of a briefcase in my head and I'm seeing the... south tower...I think it is."

"Is it south darling?" she said to Matt.

Matt nodded then lifted up his astral jumper that he'd designed himself through his thoughts and showed the medium the mark on his chest.

"Yes it's south and he's now showing me a birthmark, shaped like a bullet wound, on his chest," she explained.

Rowena went all shivery as the energy of truth rushed, like a mild but pleasant electrical current, through her body. She put her head in her hands and sobbed with the relief of connecting to him. After almost three torturous months of grieving she was finally sure that he was there and that he was okay.

"I love you Ro," he said to her.

"He says he loves you," Annie said.

Tears were welling up all over the hall. Rowena was bursting with love and loss.

"I worked like a stressed out idiot and neglected my family," Matt confessed to Annie. "And I'm sorry. I wished I hadn't."

"He really regrets not spending more time with you and his family. I can just see an image of him at his computer all the time. He says he worked too hard," Annie relayed.

"I do love them," Matt said.

"He does love you all."

Even Tom, now the cool fifteen-year-old, was finding it hard not to cry.

"I'm getting a picture of a hotel in New York...he says you will know...I don't know what happened here but he's really sorry and wants you to forgive him. He's really, really sorry about this, whatever it is."

Rowena nodded and managed to say the words "I do." Two words that had meant so much to Matt when she uttered them all those years ago and now, just as powerfully, those same two words meant just as much and more, as they would release him from his own prison of remorse. If Rowena could forgive him then it was easier for him to forgive himself.

Matt wanted to be as close to Rowena as possible and found his way to the back of the audience to hold her hand. Annie could see him clearly.

"He's holding your hand," Annie told Rowena. "Can you feel him?"

Rowena turned her attention to her hand. She could feel a tingling sensation.

She nodded. Delilah, who was also with her, was pleased at Rowena's psychic perceptions.

"Praise the lord," Delilah cried.

In her head Rowena was saying, "Matt I miss you so much. I miss you so much. I wish you were still with us. I miss you so much" and Matt could hear it.

"I miss you too," Matt responded. "And I love you. I love you so much. I love you and I'm so sorry."

"He misses you too and loves you," he keeps saying over and over Annie said.

Healing was taking place for both of them. This could be seen in their auras as the murky colors started to transform and become more vibrant. Rowena's hand started tingling again as Matt held it tight. This is a technique spirits can use to let their loved ones know they are still there. I used to do it to Win but she didn't know it was me, she just thought she had a funny hand because one of her dogs had licked it.

Next Matt turned his attention to his children.

"Please tell Jake that he *can* hear me," Matt requested.

"Which one of you is Jake?" Annie asked.

"That's me," Jake said shyly.

"Your dad says that you can hear him."

"I know that, it's everyone else who doesn't believe me," he said making the audience laugh.

"One day this could be you standing on stage," she annouced.

Jake was beaming.

"Jake, I'm so proud of you, you're really special," Matt praised.

Before Annie could even respond Jake said, "Thanks dad."

"What did he say?" Tom asked.

"He said that he was proud of me and I'm special," Jake replied.

"He's definitely making it up," quipped Tom.

Rowena looked at Annie for confirmation. She nodded raising her eyebrows at the same time.

"He says *you* are connected to that young lady over there." Annie pointed to Tom then glanced in the direction of Laura Johnson.

Tom was a little embarrassed but also pleased his dad was interested and still supportive of his love life.

"He's also very proud of you and loves you too. And just because you can't hear him doesn't mean he's not there looking out for you. You're special too. Okay?"

Tom nodded.

The final person he had to address was his mom. There she was in the room holding Tom's hand much to his further embarrassment listening to all that was being said. She occasionally wiped a tear from her eye and hoped that I might say something too.

"He's acknowledging you. Are you his mom?" Annie asked Win.

Win nodded. "I pray to Jesus that he didn't suffer too long in that building," she said pushing Misty's nose further back into her coat for fear of her being spotted.

"No I didn't suffer. I didn't even realise I was dead until I was a long way out of the tower," Matt explained.

Annie relayed his message.

Everyone in the audience was surprised and didn't understand how anyone could not realise they were dead. They would when they died

238

because it's not really that much different at first. While Annie explained that to the audience I asked Matt, "Have you seen anyone else you know out there?"

"No, don't think so," Matt replied.

"Look again son."

Matt looked around the room until his focus landed once more on Laura Johnson. In the aisle, beside her, stood a guy wearing suit pants, a white shirt and a green Macy's tie. Matt's energy crashed, shocked, as he saw a face he hadn't seen for months. A little more solemn looking than it usually was.

"Brad!!!" Matt exclaimed. "It's Brad, he's here. Look he's here. Brad's here," Matt said half excited, half panicking. "Does he need help?"

Matt felt a great love for Brad even though on the Earth plane he'd found him a little irritating.

"No he's fine," I reassured him. "He's here for the same reason you are."

"Sorry ladies and gentlemen Matt has just spotted someone he knows. He is telling me his name is Brad."

Brad looked up attentively. Matt made his way into the audience over towards him.

"Brad," Matt said. "It's me Matt."

Brad looked straight at him. "Matt? Hey man. How you doin' buddy?" he said surprised. "I didn't know you were..."

"You owe me a beer," Matt joked, referring back to one of the last conversations they'd had.

"I sure do. It's so good to see you," Brad embraced Matt. They hugged for what felt like ages. Something they would never have done in their Earthly lives.

"I love ya man," Matt admitted. "What about this life after death thing. It's so awesome isn't it?"

"Yeah but I'll feel happier when I get through to my family. It's been painful," Brad confessed glancing over towards his family members who were looking upset.

"Know exactly what you mean, buddy. But it'll be just fine. Don't worry."

Annie described Brad to his family and the reunion he'd just had with Matt. This was the confirmation they had come for and a tearful few moments followed. Brad gave his messages and a huge burden was lifted from both his side of reality and theirs.

"There's another, older gentleman here who claims you were married," she said now returning to Win.

"Jonathan?" Win questioned in absolute astonishment that after more than twenty years she could have some kind of contact with him.

"Yeah it's me," I said as I moved forward into the medium's aura.

"Yeah," confirmed Annie. "He's here."

"How do I know it's him and not the devil?" she asked. A smile spread across myself and Matt, who knew exactly what I was thinking. We both loved her ways so much.

"You have him in a wooden box in the display cabinet and you talk to it every day," Annie proved.

"The day I died you'd just made a blueberry pie and you've never been able to make it since," I reminded her.

Annie repeated the message, almost repeating it word for word. Win knew that no-one could possibly know that. She was now wiping tears quite frantically from her face, not wanting to appear too upset in front of her grandchildren.

"Win, I love you still after all these years," I told her.

"He wants you to know that he loves you and he's proud of you. He's often with you at your apartment…or when you're out and about just checking that you're okay…and when you do talk to him he can hear you…he does talk back but you can't hear him…Misty can though, he says."

Win laughed a little. She was half smiling, half crying, which kinda distorted her face a bit.

"He says one day you'll meet again and he'll be there to greet you when you pass over, along with Molly….and…Flopsy. I presume they're your dogs."

This made everyone laugh except Win who cried even more at that thought.

I knew this was a turning point in Win's life, however, and that talking to me would release a huge amount of trapped energy and emotion which she'd been carrying for years. This release would also free me because by hanging on to all this grief she was holding part of me back too.

The medium's body was getting tired now. She had to switch off. Her guide told us both to wrap it up and say our farewells. Both myself and Matt stood in her aura for one last time and projected our goodbyes and our love to our family.

"Matt and Jonathan have to go now. They're telling me to tell you that they love you all and to stay strong and look after each other. And remember that they're never ever very far away."

My family looked at each other and felt an overwhelming urge to stand up and hug one another in a circle. As they did that myself, Matt, Delilah and all the other spirit guides joined in hugging our Earth friends and family and a circle of golden light, from the higher realms, surrounded and blessed us all.

11:00PM

Later that night, Rowena was lying on the bed holding her hand out for Matt to take energetically, staring at the wedding photograph on the bedside table. Next to the picture was **The Earth Guide Book**.

"Go on pick it up," Delilah encouraged her.

Within a few seconds she'd picked it up.

"You're getting good at this game," I smiled at Delilah.

"Yeah, she's very receptive, my Rowena you know. She and I communicate all the time," Delilah replied feeling proud of her progress.

"So tell me," Rowena said talking to the book. "What's this thing called life all about then?"

She flipped it open and read,

"To grow, develop and learn how to love, whilst having an amazing human adventure, in preparation for the next world."

ACKNOWLEDGEMENTS

A big thank you to David James who created the angel behind the New York skyline on the front cover. (Check out his work at *www. emmanuelst.com*).

It is truly stunning.

Thank you to all the people who have had an input, at some point, during the creation of **The Angels of 9/11**. Including Susie Hudson (my mother, who has been full of limitless amounts of encouragement and practical help not just throughout this project but throughout my entire life), Ruth Langford (who *is* an angel in human form!), Emma Adams, Graham Sunderland, Rachel Melton (I'm so glad we share the same building), Karen Taylor, Roberta Hudson and Ken Blower.

I would also like to acknowledge all the people who were involved with the 9/11 disaster. I know you are being constantly reminded, by the media, of a day you would like to forget and I hope you can forgive me for being guilty of that too, as I pass on these messages of hope and love to the world.

All the characters in this book are fictional.

ABOUT THE AUTHOR

After graduating with a Business and Media degree Caitlin Walsh worked in environmental public relations in Sydney, Australia. On her return to Northern England, aged 24, she set up a healing practice which she has been successfully running for the last ten years.

Caitlin has also studied screenwriting at the Northern Film School.

ISBN 1-41205527-X